Swarm Magic

Other Series by Sarah K. L. Wilson

Dragon School

Dragon Chameleon

Dragon Tide

Bridge of Legends

Tangled Fae

Empire of War & Wings
Book 4

Sarah K. L. Wilson

Published by Sarah K. L. Wilson, 2020

HIVE MAGIC
First Edition. November 14, 2020

ISBN : 978-1-7772645-3-6
Cover Art by Luciano Fleitas
Written by Sarah K. L. Wilson
www.sarahklwilson.com

For Cale, always.

N
W
E
S
GLORIOUS INGV

FORBIDDING TAKEN LANDS

FAR REACH

VLAREN

KARKATUA

GVAR

FAR STONES

A COLONY OF THE WINGED EMPIRE

PREVIOUSLY IN THE WINGED EMPIRE

The crown prince took all the weapons from the people of Far Stones and they had no way to defend themselves from the dark magic that lurks there, killed Aella's father, claimed she was his property and married her in absentia. He is tied to Aella through the healing honeycomb her bees put into him and now through a magic binding that came with that wedding.

Aella was meant to Hatch into someone who manifests a magic bird but she Hatched bees instead. Her allies are Zayana, Osprey, and Ivo.

But Osprey is linked to the crown prince through magic and he's bound to stop any moves made against the throne. And Aella's best attempts to free him from this bond have failed.

Ivo has drawn Aella in to be part of a secret revolution – a revolution that he and Osprey have already committed to. Aella's family – unbeknownst to her – are all part of the revolution already.

The crown prince has a spooky power – snake magic. And spooky allies with snakes of their own. But when he offered Aella in his place for their ritual, she learned a lot of their secret knowledge that comes back to her in flashes. And now that she's been to some of their secret places, her knowledge of what is going on in the world is growing.

Aella can send her bees to buzz around someone and bring back little visions of what they are up to. She left one with the snake people and sent one to watch over her family.

She fled the city of Glorious Ingvar with a captured Osprey and there are Wings hunting them both.

And that's what you need to know.

BOOK ONE

Hope that flies,

Hope with wings,

Make us cry!

Make us sing!

Free our hearts to love again.

Show us where, and how, and when.

- *Songs of the Far Stones*

CHAPTER ONE

Hiding was our only option. My heart pounded as I tried to maneuver Osprey to a safer place inside the line of willows surrounding the farmer's field, but he couldn't hold his own weight. Without my bees and their power, he was too heavy for me to carry. It was all I could do to break the worst of his fall onto the sweet-smelling grass ringing the field.

I glanced up at the sky. The spirit-birds wings shimmered as they raced toward us from the city. With every flap of their wings, my heart seemed to speed up. Like real birds, they'd have uncommonly good vision. Which meant I had seconds to do something to hide us.

With the moon so bright, it was too easy to see everything around us, and the fires from the city made it worse. I prayed for clouds to come and cover the sky as I grabbed Osprey under the shoulders and tried to drag him across the grass. The scent of growing things filled my nose, mixing with my fear.

He was too heavy – all muscle and bone. I lost my balance and fell onto my bottom in the crinkly grass.

Forbidding take it!

My breath was coming too fast. I needed a solution right now.

We were so close to the bending willows. If I could get him under there, it could really help. There was a curving row of them close by. But what good would that do if I couldn't move him?

"How did you get so heavy?" I whispered to his slack face.

But I couldn't be angry with him.

Maybe I could roll him over the planted field and into the willows. Gripping his shoulder, I shoved him over. He flopped, rolling to his belly. I did it again and again, huffing as I worked. I had moments to get him hidden. Only moments before both of our lives would be forfeit. Oh, we wouldn't be killed, but serving at the pleasure of Le Majest was worse than death – for both of us.

I gritted my teeth and tried not to think about it, but the worries wouldn't stop.

I would not let him be dragged back to his half-brother. Not when I'd sacrificed so much already to try to save him. I had a feeling, as the warm breeze brushed over me, and the willows began to sway, that this was only the beginning. What had felt like a nearly impossible gamble would only be the start of the magic I'd have to work to free us both. We were more deeply entangled in the plots Juste was weaving than something stolen by the Forbidding. We were both enmeshed in plots within plots and schemes that would rock the Empire.

I rolled Osprey one last time and lifted the drooping branches of a willow up and over to cover him. Gasping in desperation, I scrambled to gather heaps of old dried grass and fallen willow branches from the sides of the field to heap over him. They were soft and ragged after a winter on the field, but the farmer must have cleared them recently, and they were drier than I'd expected. They wouldn't be comfortable to wait under, but they would keep out prying eyes – I hoped.

I heard a cry like an eagle in the distance and shot a glance to where the spirit-birds were in the sky.

I had to be faster.

I tried to still my shaking hands and force them to work as I frantically piled grass over Osprey, arranged the willow branches to make it look like a natural pile of branches and grass waste, and then dove for cover, wriggling to slide into the tiny hollow where I'd left my friend.

We'd have to wait here for at least a few hours – I didn't know how long – but long enough that the Wings would decide there was nothing here. And then we'd have to move again. I didn't dare remain still for long enough to be caught – and now that I was the wife of Le Majest, he would only redouble his efforts to hunt me down and have me dragged to his side. I tried not to think about what that would mean for me. I tried not to shudder or imagine the ways he would torture me now that I belonged to him in every legal sense.

I wiggled in a little close to Osprey, savoring his warmth as my arm slipped around him to hold him close and keep him still.

What did it mean to be married to the future emperor? How long would he keep me alive now that he'd tied me to him? I didn't imagine that it could be very long, despite the things he'd said about needing me. I knew Juste too well to think he'd saddle himself with me if he didn't think he could dispose of me quickly after he got whatever it was he wanted. Maybe it was just the memories from the Hissan. Or maybe it was just my quick death he was after.

I had barely finished hiding us under the dried grass when the sky above us began to grow brighter and brighter. I wrapped my arms around Osprey and tried to will myself small.

Be small, Aella. Be small. Be small.

I was nose-to-nose with Osprey. I could feel his breath gusting over my face. He moaned softly and I clenched my teeth. Had the bird above us heard it? Had he?

Something hurt in my chest – likely fear – but I clung to him. I could feel his warmth through his trousers and mine where our legs touched all the way across the length of my left side.

Carefully, inch by inch, I moved my arm up so that my hand could cover his mouth. Just as he began to moan again, I clamped my hand over the sound.

"Shh." I tried to be gentle and as close to silent as I could be.

I was sweating now, the air chilling me as it blew over us on the cold ground. I fought against my own body – forcing myself not to shiver – as the air grew brighter yet. I couldn't bear it anymore. My eyes opened and I caught sight between the willow branches of the spirit bald eagle circling above us. Its claws nearly scraped the willows above me, its orange glow bathing the fields in light. It circled, gave another cry, and then started to ascend again.

I slowly let out a breath of air, grateful for the descending darkness.

Before I could even relax, new light hit me – thick and bright pink like a summer rose. I held my breath as the new light flooded the field. Would each of them make a pass? I was shaking from the tension and the cold, willing myself to be still, while trying to listen to Osprey's breath. Was he still breathing? My bees hadn't killed him, had they?

No, his breath was still warm on my hand.

The pink glow faded, and I relaxed into the darkness, letting my hand fall from Osprey's mouth and letting my body sink into his. It felt like an invasion of his privacy – especially when he was unconscious. But there was only so much room in this little hollow, and I was getting colder by the moment. Maybe he'd be grateful to be warm if he knew what was happening.

I huddled next to him, trying to keep still as one bird after another passed over us. I thought there must be an end to them eventually, but as night deepened, it only seemed to go on and on. My heart beat wildly and the only way to calm my breath was in the memory of that kiss, so sweet and so overwhelming all at once. That might be the only time I ever felt like that. Especially now that I was married to Juste. Would Osprey still want to kiss someone who had married his brother – even if it was against her will? Maybe not. And that made it all the more special.

I felt that familiar sick sensation every time I remembered how I'd been married against my will – my agency violated, my freedom stolen. I waited for the nausea to pass.

We were so vulnerable here – just a heartbeat away from our lives being over. The moment I stepped out of this tangle of willows, one of these birds would see me and in hours the Wings and Claws would descend on me and drag me back to their lord and master to be caged until I died as his wife. Juste had told me himself that if that happened, I would never leave his side. I would remain there – forever tortured – until my life leaked away.

But at least I'd have this one warm memory filling me with remembered heat until then. And I'd have this stolen night beside Osprey. I tried to remember every detail. To treasure every moment here at his side, resting in his warmth, close enough to touch him almost as if he were actually mine instead of utterly unattainable. And as I lay there, I pled for his life to the skies and stars. It felt as if my prayer went up and up past even the skies, past even the ever-watchful stars to whatever lay beyond. And if there was some great being beyond, then I prayed that he was real and that he would listen and give Osprey the faith to keep fighting.

I pressed my cheek against the cloth of his jacket, letting the softness of the wool and the embroidery contrast with the scratch of the willow branches and grass surrounding us.

As the hours passed, his breath grew more and more labored, his chest heaving with every breath drawn in, and there was nothing I could do but shed hot tears, remain still, and plead to whatever lay beyond for healing, that the wrongs done to him might finally be made right. That justice might be possible.

I could feel my bee working in him – just under the surface of his skin, burning hot and bright and working, working to slowly take in and digest the tangles of Forbidding that bound him. It was drawing energy from me in a thin stream that I could feel as it leaked out. That was fine. He could have all my energy. He could have all of me if it could help. Give it to him, please.

There was a heat in my chest and a series of pains radiating from the feather in my chest that made me think he really was taking some part of me.

But if anyone or anything heard my prayers, there was no answer. And as the first rays of morning light finally tainted everything with a dull hue, my heart sank. It was light now. And I still had no way to run and without that, no better way to hide.

The feather in my chest grew heavier and hotter by the moment. I let my hand reach up and press against it, trying to hold in the pain that made my eyes smart with tears. I tried to think of physical things to ground me. My hair was in my eyes. Osprey's breath stirred it – especially when he was agitated in his sleep and it gusted out a little rougher. My neck was getting sore from being pressed against his chest at an awkward angle. The air was cool, and my breath felt moist compared to it. The grass smelled of summers past. Every detail helped keep me there in that moment instead of worried.

A vision rocked me, and I was looking from the honeycomb in Juste's belly, watching a grizzled Claw with wings of white in his tightly curled black hair listening silently and grim-faced as Juste spoke to him.

"… a state of martial law in every city of Far Stones. It's the only way to prevent this from happening in other places. We must restore order and the law, General. We must ensure that our people thrive in peace and tolerance. Send birds to every city. No one is to be out of their homes past dark on pain of death. No one should leave their homes for anything other than strictly necessary supply trips and those should be direct and brief. We must have cooperation from everyone if we're to ensure order. Do you understand?"

"As you say, Le Majest. And the rioters?"

"Round up those you can find. We will execute them in the morning."

I blinked back to reality and found myself shivering and not just from the cold.

At least the spirit-birds weren't soaring overhead as often. When there was a break from them, I whispered strong words to Osprey and to my bees, hoping for healing for both of them, for strength. For endurance.

"Be relentless," I begged them. "Be more than others think you are. You do not need to be bound. You can fly free."

My words rang hollow in my ears. I was such a failure. I'd

failed to save my dad or my family from the crown. All my bold words, and I'd failed to save myself. The general I'd risked everything for was insane. Ivo was very ill. My brother and Zayana were stuck caring for both of them. The revolution had started – but the wrong way. If I'd just followed Ivo and Osprey's lead, maybe that wouldn't have happened. And I'd taken this big huge gamble that I could save Osprey and that had failed, too. I was failure upon failure upon failure and the thought of that stung deep.

And now I was branded, tied to Juste, and thoughts of him made my belly clench and ache. I felt like I might be sick. And at the same time I felt guilty, as if he had stained me somehow by marrying me and made me unfit to be lying here next to Osprey or kissing him last night, and the more I thought about it the more the shame of who I was now tainted that beautiful memory of Osprey's soft lips against mine, of his gentle sigh and glorious eyes and I felt empty and aching.

Empty and lost and scared and aching and aching and aching.

Even with the dawn, the constant surveillance of the spirit-birds didn't end. My muscles began to cramp from tensing and fear. My head began to spin from worrying so much. If I didn't move soon, they would send Claws on foot to sweep out from the city, and then how would we escape? If I didn't move soon, I'd go crazy from second-guessing double-thinking everything that had happened. If I didn't move soon, it would be too late. And yet I couldn't leave Osprey here. He muttered and moaned, tossing irritably now that dawn had come.

I bit my lip and watched him, worried about how the pain might be affecting him. I reached out to my bee inside him and felt the hum of it resonate through me. With it, came a sense of healing and warmth and the feeling as if a warm thread reached from me to the bee, drawing from my strength and health to fuel the work the bee was doing. I let out a long breath. At least it was trying.

A vision rocked me, and I clenched my eyes tight, hoping I wouldn't see Juste. I didn't want to even think of him.

What I saw was Ixtap. He and his men sneaking up a rocky shore in the early rays of dawn. They were dressed oddly in plain clothing decorated with embroidery and feathers. It was almost as if they were pretending to be regular Far Stones people – rather than our enemies. But why would they do that? One look at their snake-marked faces, tattooed with the creatures they so loved, and into their hate-filled eyes – should be enough to tell anyone they were not from our lands. I clenched my fists as they stopped a cart on the road, but I couldn't look away from the vision, not even when they ripped the carter from his cart, slit his throat, and left him in the bushes on the side of the road. My bee buzzed in agitation, zipping here and there so hard that I lost the vision and almost lost the contents of my stomach with it.

I lay back, gasping as I fought against nausea until movement disturbed me. Osprey struggled, wordlessly, thrashing against the branches for a moment.

"Shh," I urged him, placing a gentle hand on his shoulder as I pushed myself up to one elbow. "Quiet."

He moaned, his teeth gritted, and eyes screwed shut.

Urgently, I looked up through the willows and around us. I didn't see any pursuers in the area, but that didn't mean they weren't close.

"Osprey," I whispered. Perhaps I could wake him enough to get him on his feet. We needed to leave. It would have been better to be running hours ago, but even running now was better than nothing.

His only answer was a gasp, the dark fringe of his eyelashes fluttering against his cheek.

"Os –" I started to say and then his eyes snapped open and his hand shot out and he pinned me to the ground, flipping me under him so quickly that I couldn't catch my breath.

"House Apidae," he growled, low and deep. "You must not let me get the upper hand like this, for it compels me to bring you to your husband."

The aching sadness in his eyes was completely at odds with the powerful way he held me in place under him, his eyes roving over my face as if he was drinking in the very sight of me.

"You should not have unbound me," he whispered.

And he was right. I couldn't squirm out from under him. He was too heavy. Too strong. And now I was trapped. The moment he pulled us from this willow tangle, we'd be seen by his allies and dragged to the heart of his brother's court.

I opened my mouth to beg him to stop and then his eyes rolled back into his head and he collapsed on my chest with a groan. He was so heavy that it was all I could do to catch my breath and wriggle my way out from under him.

Well. I sucked in a relieved breath, smoothing my wild hair back from my face.

I was lucky he was still so weak, wasn't I?

I ran a hand through my hair, gathering my thoughts, and then, with care, I rebound his eyes and hands and checked to make sure our tangle was still intact enough to hide us from sight.

This was going to be much more complicated than I'd imagined.

CHAPTER TWO

When Osprey moaned himself awake a second time, I was ready. I'd done as he asked and trussed him up like a captive.

I gently stroked his face as he was coming back to consciousness, wincing at the scratches on his face that he'd acquired as I'd rolled him into this tangle of willows. He'd been scratched again, just now, when I'd had to manhandle him to bind him again.

I could feel his panic at being bound and blindfolded in the rapidness of his breathing. It calmed after a moment and he whispered.

"Still you, House Apidae?"

"Still me."

"Are we being hunted by Le Majest?" His voice was husky.

"By his Wings. It's midday. They searched all night and we've barely managed to stay hidden. Do you think you can stand? The Forbidding has been cleared from these fields, but if we work our way into the forest, we should eventually find it, and then we can hide in the tangles of infected land."

"Infected?" he asked.

I shrugged before I realized he couldn't see it. "If there's a tendril of Forbidding inside of you and the feather is tied to it, then wouldn't that mean you've been infected? And maybe that means the land is infected, too."

"I wasn't exposed to this dark magic until well after I had the feather put into me, House Apidae," his tone seemed to be fighting off both exhaustion and pain.

"It claims to have a root in all of us," I said, my hand wandering up to my collarbone and the blazing pain just under it where my own feather begged me to return to its master. It seemed to hurt more when I edged toward Osprey, as if it hated him in the same way that Juste did.

Osprey grunted.

"Can you stand, with my help?" I asked, biting my lip.

"For you, I will try," he said, shortly, his breath gusting painfully as he flexed his muscles and moved up to a kneeling position with his hands still bound before him. I quickly stood, working to part the willows and rip extra branches from above him. Part of me was hopeful at his movement and another part terrified. We were exposed now. Anyone could see us here.

He was pushing up to his feet before I had the space clear and I dropped the branches in my hands to grab his elbow and steady him. He leaned into me, and at first, I thought he was too weak to stand, until I realized he'd leaned his cheek tenderly to the top of my head, like a hug without his arms.

"Osprey?" I said in a small voice.

"Mm?" He sounded preoccupied.

"I should have told you what I was going to do. I should have asked if you wanted to take this gamble instead of taking it for you."

"Come now, House Apidae, one night in cold and terror and you're already renouncing your kidnapping and repenting of forcing your magic into me?" He murmured the words into my hair, a hint of humor in his voice. "You smell of spring grass, and fresh breezes, and new tomorrows."

I felt my cheeks grow hot. "It's not right for me to gamble with your future."

His laugh was husky. "My future has been gambled again and again, passed from hand to hand until I'm surprised there's a scrap of it left. If anyone should gamble with it now, should it not be the one who owns me heart and soul? But you should leave me behind, House Apidae. I can feel your bee at work – feel it sifting through my being and building something new within me. I know the bee has a long range and you can flee without me. If I'm found, there is little they will do to me beyond sending me after you again, but if they find you, all our hopes are lost. If you must gamble, then toss me aside and bet on yourself."

I took his arm and began to lead him from the tangle we'd shared all night, deeper into the thick brush. I couldn't stop the branches from clawing at his face and bare skin, but at least his eyes were protected.

"If my bee succeeds, wouldn't that take away your protection? Why would your brother leave you alive without whatever this bond is that holds you?"

He shook his head and that was all the answer I needed. He might be very brave, but he was not invulnerable. When the feather was gone, Juste would have no reason to keep him alive. We both needed to escape.

"Whatever you do," he said, "you must not unbind me. I cannot yet call Os. My head is spinning, and it is hard to keep my feet and thoughts straight. But if I have even a tiny bit of willpower, I am still bound to return you to your new husband." He almost seemed to choke on the word. "You must not allow that. Keep me bound. Keep me blindfolded, so that I cannot use Os to overpower you, even if I can call him. I cannot fight what I cannot see. I trusted you, House Apidae. Now you must trust me – and follow my advice."

I looked anxiously around me, wishing there were more options to get him away from here – a likely river with a handy boat in it, or a road with friendly travelers, or even a barn to hide in. But there were none of those things. So where to? Too bad we weren't closer to the undertrails. I didn't think I could find my way back to them from here without swinging closer to the city and that would mean capture.

I shuddered. I must not be captured. He must not be captured.

"Don't fear, House Apidae," Osprey said gravely. "If anyone can keep away from the strike of the snake, it's you and your bees."

I was grateful he couldn't see my face. I was certain my expression would show all my doubts.

"Come on," I said gently. "We can't stay here."

I led him through the forest, keeping to game trails and little forest paths so I wouldn't get lost. We were still hidden partially by treetops above, but at least this way we weren't completely in the open but also not completely wandering through thick woods.

What would be worse? Getting lost with no belt knife, no water or food and no way to survive alone, or being found by the Wings?

"Have you thought through a plan?" Osprey asked.

"I plan to not get caught." I had no plan.

"That's the whole plan?" His mouth formed a wry smile.

"We can't go back to the city, so I can't get the horses Retger left at the inn," I said, explaining my logic in a low tone as I led him through the woods. It was hard to keep my eyes on everything at once – on his feet to keep him from tripping, on the sky where the Wings might be hovering, all around where anyone might notice and say something. "I refuse to steal one – and even if I wanted to, I haven't seen any to steal – so that leaves us with our own feet and any coin we have. I only have our weapons and a single silver piece with me right now. Everything else was left in my saddlebags."

He grunted in agreement. He didn't have his usual pack with him. He must have stashed it somewhere before coming for me in the monastery – or lost it. But that didn't seem like him.

"We should not enter the Forbidding, Aella," he said to me gently. "As horrible as being caught by Juste Montpetit may be, suicide is not a better option and if you flee into that tangle without anyone to help you and without the aid of your bees, it will be suicide."

"What do you mean, 'without the aid of your bees?'" I asked. Could he see through his blindfold? Did he realize they were not here?

He shrugged. "You must have carried me this far with them, or you would have a horse or cart with you still. Which means they were strong enough to carry a grown man – an impressive feat. But if they were still here, you would have taken me further than this. You've run out of strength. Did you sleep at all last night?"

"Hardly," I admitted with a tight voice.

His tone seemed to soften. "You watched over me instead."

I didn't want him to feel bad about it, so I didn't reply.

"And you wore yourself out." He sounded certain. "Until you rest properly, your manifestations will continue to slip through your fingers. It takes strength and energy to maintain a manifestation – even if the actual magic doesn't come from you but from the heart of the earth and the air of the sky. You need rest before you can manifest your heart again, House Apidae."

"I'll rest when they're all off my land," I said grimly. "I'll rest when this feather is out of my chest."

"I have long loved your ferocity," he said, and his dimples showed as he backed it up with a smile.

"How did you know my bees were gone?"

He chuckled. "I couldn't feel their constant angry hum. Usually, you almost seem to vibrate with your energy and passion. But right now, you feel – lighter. Less full than usual." He paused. "You had a way to travel very quickly to Glorious Ingvar. Can you use the same method to travel away from it?"

"No," I said miserably. "The only way I could find it again would be to go back to just outside the city."

"So, we are on foot – one of us bound – and they are in the sky and all around us."

In the silence of my answer, I heard a raven shriek.

I barely made out a flash of light in the distance and then I tugged Osprey down.

"Get low! Duck!" I dragged him after me toward a fallen tree, trying to shove us both into the cover provided by the clawing roots from where they reached out searching for the land they'd lost.

He hit his head on a low branch and cursed quietly as I helped to stuff him under the shelter of the spreading branches, keeping a hand on his neck and the back of his head to help guide it under and keep him from hitting it again.

We huddled together, our breath gusting out as one while the raven flew over. Bright gold sparks shivered in the air as it swept over us. It circled a second time, lower. I tried to hunch closer, tried to make myself small, prayed in the silence of my mind.

Skies have mercy. Stars have mercy. Keep us safe. Hold us in the hollow of your hand.

The pain in my chest from just hunching so close to Osprey was intense. What was going on with this feather? I clutched my chest against the pain.

It was long minutes as the raven began to circle more broadly, centering out from where we were. My breath was still caught in my throat, aching and terrified.

"When I was a boy," Osprey whispered, "I got lost in the late afternoon. I'd been with other boys from the keep and we went far down the beach, hunting starfish. And we found a cavern that was usually full of water, but it was low tide, so we went in it together. But the cavern was dark and twisting and after running through it with the others, laughing, I soon realized I was alone – that the only voices I heard were merely echoes of my own.

"It was too dark to see and as I tried to find my way to the cavern mouth, the water rose, washing over my ankles and then my knees. Frantic, I searched for the way out but only grew more lost, more panicked. Eventually, I found a place to scramble far up into a hollow tucked high up in the rock and I waited and waited there until the water was so high that it brushed the soles of my feet and my bottom as I sat hunched as high as I could go. I waited for it to drown me. And I prayed to whatever is beyond the sky to watch over me and see me to the other side.

"It was a very long time to sit shivering and gasping and hoping. And when, eventually, the water receded, I crept down again, and I heard a voice calling my name and a light swelled into the caverns, and there was my mother. She scooped me into her arms and carried me all the way home, half-sobbing and half-telling me how precious I was to her and how she would never lose me again."

I felt for his hand with one of mine and took it, while I pressed a finger to his lips. The bird was overhead again. Circling. Circling. Soon, the Claws would be here, too. It was only a matter of time. My heart was racing as I pressed closer to Osprey. My eyes following the large spirit-bird above. Would I have the strength to fight when eventually we were found? Would my bees be back to full strength by then?

It felt as if we, too, were deep in that cavern, lost together. But Osprey's mother was not coming for us. I would have to be there for him right now.

Beside me, Osprey swayed lightly, and he leaned on me with more weight than I thought he would if he was fully well.

My heart was still thundering as the raven finally flew away again. I removed my finger from Osprey's lips.

"House Apidae?" he whispered.

"Yes?"

"You are the one so precious to me that I would walk any path to save you, face any danger to find you, pay any price to keep you from harm. When this feather has left me, I will prove that to you."

"I don't need to be safe," I said. "I need to be free."

"I know," he said, and he leaned in a little closer so that his face was tucked in the hollow of my neck. He kissed me there, almost reverently. "I will honor that."

I hesitated. "Vasyklo?"

He shivered slightly at my use of his name.

"House Apidae."

I reached up and cupped his face with my hand and in response, the feather in my chest seemed to almost stab me with pain. I bit my lip against it and shivered a little when he leaned into my hand, his rough stubble chafing my palm.

"Are you – are you upset that I am married? Does it make you hesitate about me?"

"I don't think you're married, House Apidae. Did you say vows?" His voice was deep and burred.

"No."

"Did you commit yourself before the stars and the skies?"

"No."

"Then it's very simple. You are not married at all." His tone was almost light.

I helped him up from the tangle we were hidden in, half-pulling him up when he seemed to sag at the effort. My feather burned in my chest.

"I am in the eyes of the law."

"A law that we plan to overthrow. You want to be free? I want you to be free, too. Free of oppression. Free of evil. Free of a man who would take you against your will. And I will give my life and all that I am to give you that. But House Apidae, can you lend me a little strength? I think I'm almost out."

I was already letting him lean on me. What else could I do? I wondered. An image of his mother, gathering a young Osprey in her arms came to me and I shifted so I could wrap my arms around him in a hug. I could feel his sigh in my hair. Gently, I reached for his face with both my hands, and when he pressed into them rather than pulling back, I leaned in and slowly, gently, kissed him. Kisses, it turned out, only became more addictive the more you had of them.

Even when every one of them sends a stab of pain from that marriage feather into my heart. My head was spinning, and nausea rolled up through me before I was finished and I had to break away – gasping and trembling – before the pain left nothing but a dull ache behind.

"I need to find you somewhere safe to rest before your strength fails," I whispered.

"Keep kissing me like that and I might just fly without Os." But his whisper wasn't entirely honest, and he leaned on me heavily as I helped him along the forest floor.

I felt an almost wiggling feeling in my mind and then he stumbled beside me. I caught his arm, but I knew what it was by instinct. My bee was going deeper. It was burning out more of the Forbidding inside him.

He was swaying badly by the time I found a path and began to follow it through the trees. It would be safer to go deeper into the forest, but I needed somewhere to hide – somewhere warm and safe – and that meant people.

I should have had a better plan than this – but I hadn't expected to kidnap him. I hadn't expected to be chased. This was all new to me.

The pain in my breast seared through again so that I clutched my chest with one fist as I tried to catch my breath. Time was limited. Eventually, either Juste would pull me to him with this feather, or I would have to set one of my bees loose on myself and hope I could maintain the strength to heal while healing myself – somehow that seemed impossible. I gritted my teeth and pressed on.

We spoke little, and despite Osprey's claims that my kisses could fuel him, I could tell he was digging deep in himself to keep himself upright. I tried to tell him stories of my own past to keep him with me. Stories of my brothers and sisters and our small adventures. Of the time Abghar had to cut my pony loose from the Forbidding with me still on its back. Of the time I'd climbed a tree and been stuck up there until Helissa brought a ladder, scolding me all the while. Of the time our cat gave birth to thirteen kittens and the troubles they caused that winter when all of us claimed one for ourselves and we found that Raquella had hidden the extra two in the attic.

I thought it must be helping, because he kept on stumbling forward, leaning often into my strength.

And all this talk of family clutched at my heart and finally set my feet on a firm path. I would bring Osprey to my family. They would know what to do next. They would help me figure out what to do about my marriage. My belly rolled at the reminder that I was married – as if being married to Juste Montpetit wasn't bad enough, this feather was making me ill for it.

I just had to find them. I whispered into my hand, thinking of it.

"Come to me, friends. Come. I need your vibrant spirits. I need your fast flight. I need your quick wits. Be like shooting stars. Be like flares of dawn. Be like the Forbidding itself – ever cunning, ever reaching."

Osprey mumbled something beside me as I brought us to an abrupt halt. Two bees tumbled into my palm and I blew on them.

"Fly fast and true," I whispered. "You must find me a safe place to bring Osprey. Look for the Single Wing. And you must find my family and guide them back to me. Fly fast. Fly true. Fly to the heart of things."

Words had power. And I hoped mine had more power than ever as my heart ached, watching them fly. Hopefully, they wouldn't be caught along the way.

"Hold on," I whispered to Osprey as I led him down the path. If my words had the power to change reality where my manifestations were concerned, maybe they could do it for Osprey, too.

As we walked and he stumbled along, leaning on me, half in and half out of reality, I talked to him again, but this time I told him how he was brave and strong and how he had tried to save me but how, in the end, I was going to save him and all the children he'd loved and cared for.

Eventually, we found an old cabin with a caved-in roof. By then, it was nearly dark, and Osprey was growing so heavy that I could barely hold him up. I stumbled through the door of the cabin, dragging him with me, and found that while the roof had collapsed over what had once been a rough-hewn table and fireplace, the old straw tick and rope bed was still intact with half a roof hanging over it.

Exhausted, I helped Osprey fall onto the tick, trying to ignore the way it rustled as the vermin in it that were hidden deeper in the straw. I sat on the edge of the bed and tried to catch my breath.

We'd made it one day alive. I had no food and the only water was likely in the mossy rain barrel I'd seen in the yard. It was curious that this old cabin hadn't been taken over by the Forbidding already, but I was hardly going to complain. In a moment, I would go draw us water from that barrel – somehow. There wouldn't be a fire. We didn't dare risk the glow or the smoke. But at least this place provided good cover from spirit-birds flying overhead, and the state of the place suggested that no one called it home anymore.

I spread Ospreys cloak out as best as I could, so it formed a barrier between him and the straw tick and then I tried to get him comfortable on the bed. He filled most of it, his long limbs sprawling in every direction and his lips parted in deep sleep. Worried, I checked over his wounds. I needed to do it before I lost the last of the light.

The wound on his chest looked the same as it had back at the monastery. It glowed faintly from my bee deep inside it and even knowing I'd put the bee there, I still shuddered at the thought of something living crawling around inside his chest.

I inspected his other wounds for the first time. The knife wounds were deep and while some were healing nicely, others were angry and red, some healing in a puckered fashion, others still open. They needed proper attention. I felt his forehead, but he seemed a normal temperature. He should be burning up with all this infection. He needed a real healer.

I shook my head as I took off the short swords and leaned them against the bed. Before I could get him what he needed, I needed sleep. I could barely keep my eyes open and while I probably could have tucked in next to him in the bed, it didn't feel right. Not even when we'd slept side by side in the tangle of willows. Too much had been done to Osprey against his will. Too many choices had been made without him. I shouldn't take this choice from him, too. He shouldn't share a bed with a woman without his permission being granted first. Even a woman barely old enough to be considered more than a girl.

I forced myself back to my feet and searched the old cabin until I found a pewter cup on a shelf. I knocked out the spider and dead flies inside, cleaned it as best as I could, and filled it from the rain barrel, trying not to think of frogs as I took my first sip and then brought a little to wet Osprey's mouth. When he woke, I'd offer him more.

I pulled my handkerchief out and tucked it around his bindings, making him as comfortable as possible and then slumped to the floor beside the bed, leaning my head against the musty straw tick. I placed one of the short swords beside me – free of its scabbard. Who knew if I might need it?

Then, I pulled the silver penny Osprey had given me out of my pocket and looked at the side with the faces of two brothers on it. Two brothers. Two opposites. They'd torn a nation in two. Would these two brothers I was so deeply entangled with do the same thing now? They were certainly ripping me apart.

I didn't think it would be possible to fall asleep so uncomfortably. But I must have been asleep because I woke with a start. Someone knocked against the rain barrel outside. And Osprey was still asleep beside me.

CHAPTER THREE

I blinked myself awake, my heart in my throat. Whoever was here must know we were here, too. It would be too much of a coincidence that two travelers would seize upon the same idea of spending the night in this decrepit shack at the same time.

Cautiously, I put my hand on the hilt of my short sword and let my head rest back against the mattress, eyes closing to slits, feigning sleep. The shadows around the bed should hide me.

Whoever it was, he was quick. He had the door open and was across the creaking floor in a heartbeat. He leaned over the bed where a shaft of moonlight from the broken roof lit Osprey's face. I heard his breath suck in when he noticed the blindfold – or maybe it was the belt binding Osprey's hands, but there wasn't time to speculate. I reached up from my place on the floor, seized the front of his shirt before he could make a move, and pulled his head down to where the tip of my short sword nicked his throat.

"I think that's close enough, don't you?" I asked, my voice barely louder than my beating heart. "How many are with you?"

"Just me," he said hoarsely. He wasn't very tall – only a few fingers taller than me – but he was wide and muscular.

"And with no light and no knock, you can only have one purpose here."

"It's not what you think." His words were hurried.

"You're not hunting fugitives fleeing Le Majest?"

"I am, bu –"

I cut him off. "Then it's exactly what I think. You're going to drop your weapons."

"Easy," he said, trying to straighten. I pulled harder on his shirt, letting the tip of my sword bite into his flesh. He hissed and he was close enough now that I could see his face clearly in the moonlight. He was in his thirties. A rough stubble lined his cheeks. His eyes were wide in the moonlight, but one drooped slightly, made heavy by scar tissue. On his temple, a single wing showed.

"What's the meaning of that tattoo?" I tried to make my voice dangerous. I didn't dare sound eager. Didn't dare even hope he might be friend instead of foe.

"You must know what the Single Wing are, girl, since your brother and a man calling himself Wing Ivo arrived on my door with hardly a welcome, yanked me from my bed last night, and set me out to search for you. Me and half the Single Wing surrounding the city. 'Just in case,' they said and yet here you are in the old Vyten cabin, camped out with a prisoner."

I eased the sword back and he straightened.

"I'm glad you've decided to let me live," he said a little sourly, rubbing his throat. "Your brother didn't mention how handy you were with a blade. We don't have much time to get you out of here as it is. The Wings have been flying around the city day and night and now Claw patrols have been sent out. Met one myself. They showed me a paper with your face drawn on it and a warning about bees."

"Is there somewhere close by that's safe?" I asked, scrambling to my feet.

"Not exactly. I'm Marcel, and until I was set to be your nursemaid, I was blacksmith of my village. Your brother said you're called Aella. Didn't mention a prisoner."

"He couldn't have known," I said. "Good to meet you, Marcel."

"Sure," he sounded put out and cranky – which he was. I hardly knew what to do with him. "Is he dead or dying? You sure as skies didn't carry that big boy all this way and he hasn't stirred since I arrived. Looks like he's bound up quite a bit. Feverish maybe."

"He's sick," I said shortly. "And I don't need a nursemaid."

"Maybe he does," Marcel said with a grunt. "I have a cart on the main road and a pony where the trail branches. I'll get the pony and we can put the prisoner on it. Unless you want to leave him here. I'm not against leaving War and Wings boys to their own fates. They took my Barla when she tried to hide her sword from them. Displayed her body as a warning."

His voice was raw now with unhealed pain and I flinched in sympathy.

"I'm sorry."

"We're all sorry," he snapped but then he seemed to recover himself. "I'll get the pony if you want to keep him."

"He's not like the rest," I offered.

"Sure," he said. "People always say that and it's never true. But I'll do as I was asked. Those fool city people might have jumped the gun but none of this works if we don't all work together."

"None of what works?"

"The revolution. Have you lost your hearing?" I waited to see if he wanted to vent more but he shook himself and sighed. "The pony. I'll be back."

I was still shaking my head as he left. He was a strange man, but if he truly had a pony and a wagon and if patrols really were on their way – and I was sure he was right about that – then he was my best hope of getting out of here.

I sat gently on the edge of the bed and tried to shake Osprey awake.

"Osprey?"

He woke slowly, swallowing, and then grimacing.

"I have water here," I whispered, helping him up enough that I could guide the cup to his lips.

He drank and then drank again and then collapsed back onto the bed.

"Apidae," he whispered, and his breath was faint.

Worried, I touched his forehead, but he was not burning up. I laid the back of my hand against his cheek and was surprised when he nuzzled against it with a happy sigh. Perhaps he wasn't fully conscious. Perhaps he was dreaming or flickering in and out of sleep. My cheeks burned hot all the same. He clearly was thinking about me, even if it was in his sleep, and I liked that very much.

Far too much.

I shouldn't be so distracted. But the bee stings on his lips were gone and part of me very much wanted to put more of them there.

Before I'd even managed to finish the thought, his bound hands came up gently and found my side, catching my jacket in his grip and very softly drawing me down to him. I leaned in, tilting my head in case he was going to whisper. I was right.

"I've been dreaming of bees and honey."

His whisper sent a little shiver down my spine.

"My mother loved honey. She used to raise bees and she'd give some honeycomb to me whenever I asked. I always find honey anywhere I visit and bring some home in her honor. I keep little jars of it in a chest in my old room at House Osprey."

He was muttering and I wasn't sure if he realized he still had my jacket in his hands, that he was telling me this story. It was possible that he was still dreaming.

His breathing changed and I wished he had no blindfold on so I could see his eyes.

"Kiss me and let me taste honey again," he whispered. "I love all those stings your bees offer me just as I love the buffeting wind that cuffs me and slaps me even as it lifts me up on the heights."

He was definitely delusional. My bee was going deeper. And yet, even now, I couldn't say no.

I leaned in and kissed him, drinking in this nearness that surely couldn't last. Whatever it was he tasted like, it was so much better than honey.

I didn't hear the door creak, but I nearly squeaked when light burst into the cabin.

"So that's the way it is," Marcel said wryly. "I ought to take you straight to the Skybinder, the pair of you, and see you married properly. But a married couple will do as a disguise. The posters don't mention that. They only mention a girl with wild hair and a tendency to sting."

He swatted a glowing bee aside, and my cheeks felt hot as I realized I'd manifested again, that Osprey had a sting on his lips again and I hadn't been able to control myself and keep that from happening. Judging by his two dimples and the way he could barely contain his laughter, he didn't mind.

"It will be hard to sell you as a married couple if he remains bound," Marcel said, throwing a pair of dark cloaks at me. "Best to untie him."

"I can't," I said, my cheeks so hot now that someone could make tea if they set a kettle onto them.

"If you need to keep him bound to keep him near then he's a poor choice, girl," Marcel replied, and I couldn't tell if he was mocking me. "A pretty girl like you can find another boy. You don't need to tie up an unwilling one – though I'll admit that it looked like he was taking as much as he was giving just now."

Embarrassment and horror welled up hot in me. "He didn't … I wasn't."

Osprey was shaking now, and I knew it was from suppressed mirth.

"At least he clearly has his energy back. Up now, lad. I know you aren't well but if you've the strength to kiss girls who like to stab anything that moves in the night, then you've the strength to get to my pony on your own two feet." He reached down and helped Osprey up. "That's right. And what name shall I call you? Lover-boy feels accurate, but a touch too much like an endearment and I'm not that kind of blacksmith."

"Os… Vasyklo," Osprey said. "And it's a pleasure to meet you, blacksmith."

"Likewise, prisoner. You're sure he needs these bonds girl?" I nodded. "Truly?" I nodded again and he shook his head. "Well, at least you got yourself entangled with a pretty one, then boy." He was already leading Osprey ahead of me and out the door, holding his lantern high while I gathered our weapons. He was far too chatty. I wished I could get help from someone – anyone – else. "Best to let her keep you, I suppose, though she's far too stabby. Think on that. Marrying a stabby girl might seem like a fun adventure until she actually draws blood."

"Oh, she's already done that, blacksmith."

Marcel clicked his tongue. "I hope these bandages aren't on her account."

"Every one of them."

Marcel glanced anxiously over his shoulder at me. "Just say the word and I'll free you boy. She's got no right to stab you and then bind you. That's not healthy. You can find a lass just as pretty with fewer teeth and less of a tendency to bite, hmm?"

"If you untie me, I'll be forced to kill her one way or another, good blacksmith, and none of us wants that," Osprey admitted. "So, keep me tied and blindfolded and we'll all be the better for it."

Marcel clicked his tongue again, scolding. "Never have I met such a bloodthirsty pair. You both should have been raised better than this, so now you'll have to listen to me, and me barely old enough for children never mind children the age of the pair of you." He began to help Osprey up onto his pony. Osprey swayed, needing to lean against the pony to gather his strength. Marcel was surprisingly gentle, holding the younger man with one hand

and the lantern with the other. The pony, for her part, munched on new shoots of grass, ignoring them both. She was fat and placid as a summer day. "No one should be mixing kisses and violence and the pair of you should be scolded for such nonsense. Kisses are promises of loyalty and love that are soul-deep. They aren't games or toys. If you were my children, I'd smack you both for your foolishness and keep on smacking you until you realized there's a soul-bond that starts with kissing and completes in the marriage bed and no fools should start it who don't mean to fulfill it. There's a giving of your whole self to another person in all that and it's no game and not something you'd play around with where an enemy is concerned."

If my cheeks had been hot before, they were as fiery as Osprey's cuff now. I stood awkwardly to the side, feeling the gift he'd given me – the one that showed he cared about me. It burned when I slid my finger in to touch it. It always burned when he was close – like the feather in my chest did.

"Who says I don't plan to be loyal on a soul-deep level?" Osprey asked, his dimples deepening as he swayed in the saddle. "Who says I'm not already willing to give my whole self to her, blacksmith?"

Marcel's expression in the lantern light was aghast. "Sit still while I tie you to the saddle, boy. I don't dare risk you falling off, not with your eyes and hands bound like that. Skies and stars, if what you say is true then she shouldn't treat you like this and you shouldn't be talking about killing her. And I, oh I should be dragging you both off to the Skybinder, middle of the night as it may be, and brother waiting for you as he may be."

"My brother is waiting?" I asked, anxious now. "He was supposed to go on without me!"

"Enough of that now," he said briskly. "We've a long way to go yet tonight and here's the lad swaying in the saddle like he might pass out at a moment's notice."

I walked to the other side of the pony and reached up to support Osprey. He really was swaying and starting to slump now that he'd used all that energy. I felt a tiredness creeping over me, too, that might have been from the energies the bee was drawing on. Or maybe I was just tired of being hunted.

Osprey slumped against me, his head lolling enough to tell me he'd passed out again. I kept pace beside the pony, propping him up.

"We need to be silent now," Marcel said as the trail moved to a fork where it widened. "There are many eyes and ears about."

I nodded wordlessly, forcing my feet to follow the path and keep pace with the pony. My lack of sleep was catching up with me and I was finding it hard to remember to pay attention to the night around me. My head bobbed as I walked as if it, too, wanted to drift off. I didn't know how much time passed, but the moon was still up when we found Marcel's cart on the road. His draft horse was tied to a tree and he stamped impatiently as Marcel and I dragged Osprey off his pony and into the back of the cart. It was loaded high with straw. We tucked Osprey under the straw, wrapping a horse blanket around him, and then buried him under enough straw to disguise him.

Marcel moved to tie the pony to the cart and he gestured to me. "Get under the straw, too, girl. You're the one we most need to keep out of sight."

I nodded my agreement and crept under the straw in the narrow cart. To get in the right place that I could be hidden meant tucking myself tightly against Osprey's side. I tried not to think about how I was married to someone else as I shut my eyes and let myself drink in his warmth, ignoring the pain in my chest, and very promptly fell asleep.

ELSEWHERE IN THE WINGED EMPIRE

General Petren stared at the tiny scrap of paper in his hands. He knew this writing – knew it like he knew his own name and yet he'd never received a message like this from this hand. Worse, he had another, similar scrap – this one worn and frayed and so water-logged that it was almost impossible to make out the writing.

The wet one was from the son of his heart – if not of his body. It read:

I beg you one thing, father, if I may dare. Take the children from the Winged Empire. Leave as soon as you read this message. Disaster comes on swift wings. – VP

The other message was even stranger because it mirrored those sentiments exactly:

Petren. You have been loyal. In gratitude, I give you this warning. Flee the Empire. Do not Delay.

There was no signature. There didn't need to be one. Klavov Petren would have known the handwriting of the Emperor of the Winged Empire no matter where he saw it. Every order he had ever received as General had been written in that handwriting.

He froze for only a moment before tucking both notes away and calling for his guard.

"Get my steward," he ordered.

He'd need a ship. Maybe more than one. And supplies. On short notice. It would cost all he had – more if he wasn't careful. And yet, to be warned by two such disparate sources. He could not ignore it. He shook his head and made the sign of the bird as he noted that two different spiders had woven webs in the corner of the room. If that wasn't a sign, then nothing could be. He must act – now – before he fell into an inescapable trap.

CHAPTER FOUR

I woke in a cocoon of warmth that I didn't want to leave. When I blinked my eyes open, I was nose-to-nose with Osprey. His breathing was not the steady, deep breathing of sleep. Warm light filtered in through the straw and little threads of steam rolled up from the wagon into the crystalline air above. The sun was hot and bright, and the wagon rumbled and bounced over the uneven roads. I hadn't even asked Marcel where he was taking us. That seemed like an oversight now, but I'd been too exhausted to even think.

The dappled light filtering through the straw made a pattern across Osprey's face. Gently. I tugged his blindfold up a little and met his bright blue eyes. His smile still caught me by surprise.

"How are you this morning?" I whispered.

"Better. I have watched the day dawn through the light and shadow of this blindfold." His voice was a bit husky. "You talk in your sleep."

I felt my cheeks growing hot. "How could you know that?"

"Only you would mutter about giving your husband to the Forbidding as you slept."

That wasn't helping with the hot cheeks. I huffed a laugh.

"I don't know how I'm going to get out of this false marriage," I whispered, my hand finding the place on my chest that still burned and burned, trying to tug me back south again. You could almost navigate by that tug. "I don't want to be married."

"You don't want to be empress?" he whispered back. "Some people might."

"You should know better than that," I jabbed him lightly with a finger. "You should know that I want nothing from the Winged Empire except to be left alone."

"I know." And he sounded like he did – in fact, he sounded like he liked it.

"And what about you?" I whispered. "Do you want to be emperor?"

"No."

"When my bees set you free, what will happen? Will it be like you have died?"

"I don't know," his voice sounded afraid.

"I know that if Juste dies, you inherit everything, which means that if you die, he inherits everything. So, if my bee breaks that tie, it might be like you have died and he will immediately inherit the kingdom. Is that possible?"

"Yes," he whispered.

"What happens if your father dies?"

"I cannot say." There was a rustle in the straw as he shifted positions.

"But you know."

"Yes."

I let that go for now. "If my bees can really set you free, what will you do?"

"I'll fight," he said, earnestness setting his face hard. "I'll fight to free you from their clutches and to free this colony. I'll be the best defender you've ever known."

"And the children?" I asked because I knew that even with the tie broken, he was going to want to save them. And how could he do that?

"There will be a way," he said grimly. "I will find a way."

We rode like that for many hours as Osprey struggled through waves of immobilizing agony followed by spells where he breathed a little easier and clutched at my hands.

Twice, Marcel let us out from under the straw for a quick break and to eat and drink. Both times he rushed us in again with worried glances the moment the sound of other travelers reached our ears. He informed us he was taking us north to a place where my brother was waiting. That was all he would say on the matter and though I wanted to press him more, I didn't. We needed his help and since he was constantly impatient with us, I was afraid he'd leave us on the road if I said the wrong thing.

And we couldn't afford to be left on the road. Marcel handed me a parchment with my description on it at our first stop. He'd found it nailed to a tree at a crossroads. The hand of my husband was everywhere and if I wasn't careful, he would snatch me up again.

"If your father dies, someone has to inherit," I whispered to Osprey when the cart started rolling again. "And if you are both alive, that would mean that Juste would inherit and the feather in your chest would kill you, wouldn't it?"

"Yes," his whisper was thready, and I couldn't tell if it was pain or my words that were shaking him up.

"That's one of the things that you fear – Juste inheriting."

"He's worse than the Emperor, House Apidae. No one realizes it. He keeps his inner self carefully hidden."

"He doesn't keep it hidden from me," I said with conviction.

"No. I suppose he doesn't."

"But if the feather is gone, and someone were to harm your father, it won't be able to kill you," I said, relieved. "Let's hope your father can avoid assassination for just a few more hours."

What I didn't say out loud was that I hoped my bee would be done in a few more hours. Instead, ignoring the searing pain that filled me, I leaned in close and gave Osprey a stinging kiss – one full of all my hopes and passions for him. And when it was done, and we broke apart gasping, I whispered my vow.

"Whatever it takes, I will sever your tie to them. I'll find a way to undo what was done to you."

"I trust you, House Apidae."

After our second stop, I was rocked almost immediately by another vision. This time, Ixtap was speaking to a man in the shadows. They huddled together in a dark passage and the man looked agitated and afraid. Which didn't surprise me at all. Ixtap made me feel both those things. I still felt them when I saw him, and he was across an ocean from me now.

I was grateful to blink back to the cart and out of the vision. Should I be worried that I was seeing so much of Ixtap? What could he be up to on the other side of the ocean? It had just been him and a few others in my visions lately and they weren't charging up hills with blades drawn. This was no invasion. So what was he doing across the sea?

The road was busy, and Marcel often called to a fellow carter or stopped for a patrol to pass by. We were careful to be silent then, but whenever there was no one around, Osprey and I talked. He spoke of the beauty of the sea. Of the children of Canat who had been brought to his home – what they were like. What their passions were. How they had slowly become his friends. I spoke of my family and the homestead I'd hoped to have one day. A place for raising horses of my own. He thought bees would be more appropriate. I laughed softly at that and was rewarded with a smile.

My chest hurt constantly. And the closer I was to Osprey, the closer it seemed to burn with pain. When I kissed him – which I did almost too often, now that I knew that I could – it hurt five-fold. I began to tense even before our lips met. It was as if the marriage feather under my collarbone was trying to keep me from him.

He was in pain, too, his face often flickering with ghosts of it as we spoke or as we lay still, hiding.

Our conversations in between his bad spells were a surprising balm in the middle of our fear and tension. One moment we'd be lying beside each other, barely breathing, stiff as boards as a Claw patrol passed on the road with their carabaos jingling with tack and their commanders shouting harsh orders. Our fingers would intertangle for shared support and our hearts would race in time with one another. And then the next moment, they'd be gone, and we'd be relaxing again, and one of us would whisper a story. Osprey – or perhaps I should be thinking of him by his real name now that we'd kissed – was surprisingly good at being a friend.

The light was fading when I asked him about it.

"Should I call you Vasyklo or Osprey?"

"Call me what you will, House Apidae." I wished I could see his eyes, but his blindfold was up – protecting us both.

"Do you have a preference?"

He paused for long moments before making a discontented sound. "I prefer neither of those. Osprey is my title – a title forged in blood and obligation. Something that binds me to the throne and Le Majest. Vasyklo is the name my mother gave me – a name for one born in treachery and betrayal. I would prefer another name, perhaps."

"Then I will think of one for you," I said.

Marcel's whisper broke into our conversation. "The path is a little way ahead. I'm going to have to leave the wagon with a friend and then we go on foot to the gap."

"What gap?" I whispered back.

"The only way to get you safe. It won't seem like it will work, but you have to trust me."

"Wait," I said but he was already putting straw over us. "I'm still not sure I can trust you if you won't give me details."

"Become sure!" he hissed.

"I think we can trust him," Osprey whispered to me. "We've come this far with him."

I wanted to answer but a vision seized me, shaking me where I lay and I had to grit my teeth to keep from crying out as the feather in my chest flared with intensity at the view. At first, I was confused, thinking I was looking at Juste from someone else's eyes, but I was still looking from the honeycomb as he studied himself in a mirror, shirtless and with his boots flung to the side. His black tousled curls were in disarray and his face was drawn and haggard. He ran a hand over it and inspected the honeycomb again in the mirror, ranting to himself through clenched teeth.

"You've put your mark into me forever, Aella of House Shrike. And I've put my mark on you. Trust me, I am looking for you, and I will find you. And when I do, you will be mine just as I have been forced to be yours. Oh, you like playing games. I see that now. And we are alike, you and me. For I, too, like to play with my supper and I will make you dance for me and then I will strip you down and take from you everything you are and everything you love and you will be paraded through the place that was once your home like a pet on a leash. No sustenance will you receive except from my hand, no affection unless I give it, no praise or comfort from any but I, and one day, you will grow to be as obsessed with me as your bees have forced me to become with you."

His lip curled as he leaned closer to the mirror. "You thought you had won, didn't you? You thought you had played me for the fool, putting me forever within your grasp with that clever series of moves – first the wound, then the healing, then the bond between yourself and my brother." He leaned his forehead against the mirror, closing his eyes and murmuring to it as if he thought I was there with him. "But oh, my wife, I can turn your every game into a victory and I will. I will match you move for move, play for play until you are utterly at my mercy.

"Don't you realize, wife, that if you manage the impossible and free him, it will only set in stone what I am trying to accomplish?"

I snapped back to reality with a shudder.

"Are you hurt somehow, House Apidae?" Osprey whispered.

"Osprey," I was more breathless than I would have liked – and much more terrified. "If I get that feather out of your chest and break your tie with Juste – would that automatically kill your father?"

It was a crazy thought. But it was a crazy bond. And something was telling me that I'd guessed right.

Osprey's silence was pregnant. "House Apidae, I –"

There was a crash beside the wagon and our mouths snapped shut. Carefully, I adjusted Osprey's blindfold. If we were attacked and we had to run, he needed to be ready.

Marcel's voice was arguing with someone – low and guttural and then two more voices joined the mix.

"We search everything," Someone was getting closer to the wagon. I put my hands on the hilts of two of the short swords in my belt. When they moved the straw, I'd need to be ready. Osprey wouldn't be able to defend himself.

There was a flash above me and the ruffling of feathers.

I nearly cursed. A spirit-bird was here. Anything I did would be reported. And then what would we do? A cart was not a fast way to escape.

Osprey reached out, his fingers finding mine as if to try to steady me.

I clenched my teeth tight, hands growing sore, I was gripping the sword hilts so tight.

Were my bees back at all yet? I couldn't feel the buzz. I could only feel my own frustration washing through me like a tide. Forbidding take it!

Marcel yelled and then there was a sound like something hitting a side of meat. The voice was closer.

"Last chance. Come out of that straw."

Something thunked beside me into the wood of the wagon bed. A sword blade stabbed through the straw and into the cart bed with enough force to make it hard to draw back. If it had been six inches to the side, it would have hit Osprey. Now was the time to act.

I launched myself up from prone to standing in a fast maneuver I'd done a thousand times while laughing and joking with my older brothers. Who would have thought it would come in handy like this?

My swords were sliding from their scabbards as I took in our situation.

Marcel was on the ground, clutching a blood-soaked wound in his head. Skies and Stars! They'd hit him hard.

There were six of them. One by the cart, dressed in his fine blue Claw coat with white embroidery. He was frozen in shock as if he hadn't really expected anyone in the straw.

Two more were standing over Marcel. One with a cosh in his hand. That explained the wound to Marcel's head.

One had his pony already untied and being taken to the carabaos where the other two Claws were mounted, keeping the powerful beasts under control.

I saw in a flash that we were badly outnumbered and in trouble. I'd have to do something bold and do it fast. I drew one sword.

"Bees," I whispered, but only one popped out of my hand,

whirling around me angrily.

"It's her!" one of the guards on the carabao yelled, pointing at me.

Forbidding take it! I needed a better plan.

I reached down, grabbed Osprey by his bound hands, and pulled him up, putting my sword tip to his neck.

"This is Wing Osprey, sworn to Le Majest," I said in what I hoped wasn't too shaky of a voice. "And I'll slit his throat right here if you don't give me one of those carabaos and back off."

It wasn't much of a plan, but what other choice was there? I knew I couldn't fight six Claws. Above us, a raven screamed, its semi-transparent gold spirit body floated over us. It was going to come down for the kill, wasn't it? I could sense it the moment before it happened.

"The eye," I whispered to my bee. "Go for the eye."

The Raven dove toward us, screaming. It was a big one. Large enough to grab us both and carry us away. I ducked, pulling Osprey down with me. The raven's talons were outstretched, reaching for us, inches away.

I gritted my teeth, lifted my sword to fight, and then my bee hit the eye of the raven and it screamed again, flapping violently and rolling to the side, trying to dislodge the bee from its eye. It tumbled into a tree and then another.

I didn't wait for the fall to end. I grabbed Osprey by one arm.

"Now, we jump," I said to him and then leapt – with him beside me. We landed side by side on the ground and I pulled him past the stunned Claws toward Marcel. "Lean down and help Marcel up."

Osprey struggled, stumbling as his bound hands made it hard to lift the older man. He tugged him up and Marcel swayed, leaning heavily into Osprey.

I kept my sword close to his neck as he worked.

"None of you move," I said grimly. "He's close to Le Majest. Some might even say they are like brothers."

The Claws shifted uncomfortably, looking at one another.

"Wing Raven has seen you through his bird's eyes' by now," one of them said.

I glanced at where the Raven was shaking its head, trying to dislodge the bee. It flickered in and out.

"He's a long way off, isn't he?" I asked. "Maybe even as far as Glorious Ingvar. His manifestation is weak all the way out here."

"That won't stop him from seeing all of this and reporting it to Le Majest," the Claw said, taking a step forward. "And he wants you, girl. And no wonder with that blasphemous bee racing around your head." He made the sign of the bird. "You should be ashamed of yourself."

I pulled Osprey along as I shuffled toward the nearest carabao. "I'll work on the shame. Maybe after Le Majest shows a little shame for his own manifestation."

The Claws looked baffled.

"Now, the carabao," I reminded the rider.

"If the Wing is so valuable to Le Majest, then where's his manifestation?" One of the nearby Claws asked. They were circling around me, none of them wanting to get too close and none of them wanting to let me go free, either.

I pulled open Osprey's shirt and yanked the bandage from his wound. He hissed in pain and regret raced through me, hot and agonizing. But I kept up the bluff.

"See the stab to the heart? Have you seen that done to a Wing before? Until it heals, he won't be manifesting anything."

The Claws looked at each other, uncertainty in their eyes. And I knew I had them. They didn't dare endanger a named Wing and while they weren't sure they believed me, it was a plausible explanation.

The Claw on the carabao slipped off and I motioned to Marcel to climb up. He was in bad shape, his steps stumbling as if the earth was rolling beneath him. It took him three tries before he climbed up and I was sweating the whole time. What was I going to do with the guards when this was done? I needed some way to keep them from chasing me.

"Everyone drops the reins of their mounts," I said evenly.

They looked at each other, but they dropped the reins. They must know there wasn't much I could do. I had my hands full with trying to get Osprey up onto the carabao.

"To me," I whispered, and my bee left the fading bird. It launched into the air with a shriek. "Be strong for your size – strong and terrifying. Get these carabaos moving."

My bee was zipping from my hands so quickly that I could barely see it go, and then the pony was whinnying and then the horse grunted and all at once the cart was clattering over the ground on just three wheels, and the pony was halfway out of sight in the other direction.

The other carabao reared up, crashing to the ground so hard it sent tremors across where we stood. As he reared again, I took that moment to scramble up onto the back of our dancing carabao. He rocked his heavy horns to one side and then the other as if trying to decide which way to charge. I didn't need him to be happy, I just needed him to move. I jammed my sword in my sheath and gripped his reins, letting him have his head and chase down the road after the other trumpeting carabao.

"Hold on!" I called back to Marcel. I ducked to pull Osprey's bound hands over my head and slide them down to rest around my waist. We were uncomfortably close – well, it would have been uncomfortable with anyone else – but it was the best way I could think of to keep him safe.

"You're insane," he whispered as the carabao galloped across the rutted ground, eating up the distance in seconds instead of minutes, so very fast that I feared he might crash into something or break a leg in one of the many potholes. "You nearly got yourself captured. I've told you before that you're the priority here. If you'd left me, they wouldn't have harmed me and you would be much safer."

"It was the only thing I could think of," I said evenly.

"They know where we are now." His words were barely audible over the crashing of the carabao as it turned off the road and into the woods. My bee zipped in from out of nowhere, hovering over us and faintly lighting the wild ride.

"They knew anyway," I argued and then called back behind me. "Are you still with us, Marcel?"

He moaned. "I will be if you can slow this beast. We're going to miss the gap. It's up near a faint path ahead. I think. This animal bounces and weaves in ways I didn't expect."

"The gap you wanted to bring us to?" I asked.

"That's the one."

"The one we had to trust you about?"

"Yes."

I sawed on the reins, trying to slow the carabao, but it was spooked and angry and just like me, it saw only one way forward.

CHAPTER FIVE

We didn't miss the gap after all. Though it was not like anything I'd seen before.

The carabao eventually slowed, though it kept snorting and tossing its head in an agitated manner. The creature had run straight toward a tangle of Forbidding and the dark magic reached for it from the forest, tangling and rippling out like smoky tentacles. The carabao tossed his heavy head, horns swishing back and forth as if he could fight the landscape on his own.

A few moments after it stopped, a shape shambled out of the dark tentacles – a shape I hadn't seen since I left Far Reach. My heart stuttered in my chest.

Biting back a curse, I scrambled out of Osprey's hold and slid to the ground, drawing my sword. A Forbidding bear would make short work of a carabao. Especially one as spooked as this one.

"Grab the reins, Marcel," I called over my shoulder.

He leaned over the side of the carabao and vomited. I cursed again. I'd been right. His head wound was serious. He needed rest.

"You can't fight a Forbidding bear on your own, girl," he said in a muffled voice. He must have been wiping his mouth.

"Dodge around it and get us to the gap."

I didn't spare him a glance to look at him. My eyes were trained on the bear. I knew we couldn't dodge it and none of my companions could help me.

The bear was large for its kind. Not the largest I'd ever fought, but certainly the largest I'd fought alone – and I knew there would be no getting around it. Not with that look in its eyes. On top of that, the Claws might be right behind us if they'd managed to catch any of the mounts. I had to do this fast.

I swallowed, flexing my hand on the hilt of the sword and concentrating.

I kept my eye on the bear while I fumbled for my flint and reached down to tear up handfuls of dry grass from the base of a nearby tree.

"Stay on the mount, Marcel," I ordered him. "Whether you have faith in me or not, you're too injured to fight and someone needs to keep Osprey on the back of the carabao."

"Go through the gap, House Apidae. We will distract the bear," Osprey said, but his voice was muffled with pain. My bee must be busy again.

"Don't you dare get down from that carabao," I huffed.

I didn't look back. I'd have to hope he had enough common sense to listen to me.

The bear shambled forward, sniffing the air, its body coalescing and then disintegrating into a mass of smoky tentacles only to reform as a bear again. I kindled the fire quickly, setting it beside the tree and leaning a pile of hastily gathered sticks against the flame. I'd need it the moment I had the bear in check. Nothing killed the Forbidding except fire to the heart – unless it was maybe blood, but I had only heard about that. I hadn't seen it in action. And since cuts and wounds didn't seem to hold the Forbidding back, I could only assume the blood was life's blood – the blood of someone no longer living. And that was not an option.

The fire danced and leapt along the twigs at the same moment that the bear stood on its hind legs and lunged. I brought my sword up just in time, staying low under the charge as he crashed down on me with crushing force. It should have knocked me onto my back, but I managed a sidestep at the last second, just ducking out from under his forepaw and twisting my weight out from under him with a quick jut of the hips. His claws raked down my arm and I bit back a scream.

Behind me, I heard Osprey calling out and Marcel arguing with him. In the back of my mind, like seeing something out of the corner of your eye, I could feel my bee going deeper into his chest. No time for that.

I spun, slashing, and hacking at the bear's back. I only had time for a handful of blows. He was already twisting around, massive forearms sweeping up at me, his fingers tipped in deadly claws. I managed a spin backward, twisting my knee painfully, but just managing to dodge back from the blow. My arm was on fire from the last hit he'd scored. I didn't dare let him get another in.

Forbidding take it! He was fast. And this was so much harder on my own than it was with a brother or sister fighting with me!

He slammed against my legs and I was down, moaning, pain rippling through my legs and back. I rolled as fast as I could, careful with where I placed my sword, so I didn't cut myself. I popped to my feet as soon as I'd rolled out of his grasp, stumbling slightly on the twisted knee. It didn't want to hold my weight properly.

The fire was blazing now, and I'd popped up right beside it. I snatched one of the lit branches from the fire and brandished it in one hand, my sword in the other. I needed to end this fast. The bear was quicker than me and much, much stronger. I had only the element of surprise. My one advantage, always.

"Fly, my bee," I whispered, and I leapt toward the tangled figure just as it was in the middle of bursting apart into smoky tentacles. I thrust straight for the heart of the Forbidding tentacles, ignoring how they curled around my body, trying to snap my bones before I could plunge the fire into the heart. My sword was tangled now. My arm stuck in place.

I thrust the fire forward, but I was inches too short. The Forbidding bear roared, and as it did, the ends of it unfurled, became smoke, and then coalesced into a tangled bear again, but this time with one of my hands and swords stuck between its dark ribs. I struggled, trying to get the fire into its heart. Still too short.

The bear roared again, but this time there was a squeal in that roar. Its grip on me loosened but I didn't try to get free. I pushed toward it, instead, finally jamming the flaming stick into its heart. Flames licked at my hand, searing it as the bear went up like a heap of dry brush. Forbidding-taken things always burned hot and fast.

I stumbled backward, cradling my hand, trying to catch my breath, and fell straight into Osprey's arms. His blindfold was off, hands untied, eyes searing with relief and joy. His lips parted slightly. Was he trembling?

One of his hands held a stick like a club. He must have broken the bear's grip on me.

"You saved me," I said stupidly.

"Always," he said, smiling slightly, and then he gasped, doubling over and clutching his chest. My bee screamed in my head.

I caught him as he collapsed toward the forest floor, his face outlined in the harsh light of the burning Forbidding bear. We were vulnerable here. The Claws would follow, and the fire would light their way right to us. I had to get him out of here.

He was sucking in little shuddering breaths, shaking from head to toe. I clutched him to me as fear clawed at my heart like its own kind of Forbidding bear. I shouldn't have put my bee in him. What had I done? In my mind, the bee was still screaming, and I had the sense of something folding it, kneading it, pounding it like meat before the roasting pan.

"Hold on," I said, but I didn't know what I thought he should be holding on for. There would be no relief unless I let the bee out. We couldn't know how long it would take. We couldn't ease his pain.

His hands came up to clutch my arms and his face twisted in pain.

Maybe I should stop it. Maybe I should just let him rest.

"Don't stop it," he gasped after a moment. "I can tell you're thinking about it. Worried about the consequences. Let the bee keep working."

"What if it kills you?" I whispered. "I'll never forgive myself."

He reached into his sleeve and pulled out one of his toothpicks, his face clouded with pain as he jammed it between his teeth and scowled furiously at it.

"I'm harder to kill than you think."

"What if it triggers the death of your father and crowns your brother Emperor?"

He looked away. "We can't know that it will. Now, help me back up on the back of that beast. I don't have the strength to do it myself."

"You shouldn't have come down in the first place," I scolded him, but I helped him to his feet and took most of his weight as I helped him back to the snorting carabao. The beast rolled its eyes, but it was well-trained. Unlike Marcel. I gave him a look and he just looked right back, totally unashamed at freeing Osprey and letting him come after me. "Help me get him up."

Marcel complied, swaying as he helped me pull Osprey onto the back of the huge bull. Osprey had gone pale, sweat forming across his forehead and dampening his shirt and jacket. None of that was good. We barely managed to heave him up.

I sat there a moment when we were done, gasping for air, breathing in the scents of sweat and fire and angry bovine. My hands were shaking. Not from the bear. I'd fought Forbidding-bears before. They had a real taste for tearing horses apart so there always seemed to be one after our herd. No, they were shaking for other reasons. We all made choices. And we lived with the consequences. But could I live with having killed Osprey with my magic?

"You were supposed to keep him safe up here," I growled to Marcel. He leaned to the side and vomited again before speaking.

"I told you tying the lad up was a bad idea. See? He saved your life." Marcel had Osprey's belt. He gave me a look of defiance before wrapping it around Osprey's waist for him and buckling it. He jammed the blindfold in Osprey's pocket. Osprey barely even seemed to notice. He was chewing the toothpick aggressively, eyes focused ahead, hands gripping handfuls of his jacket as if they needed something – anything – to steady them.

I shook my head. Marcel had not helped at all. But I had two men in desperate need of care, enemies on our heels, and nowhere to take them that was safe. I heard a call in the distance. Someone had seen the fire.

Forbidding take it!

"Where's this gap, Marcel?"

"Right there." His eyes were glassy, and he was pointing to where the Forbidding tangled between the trees. There was a faint trail that led to that spot, but it looked more like a game trail than anything else.

"There's nothing there."

Behind me, there was another call, this one closer. They were on our trail.

"Either trust me that there is a gap," Marcel said, "or don't trust me and the Claws will take you to where you don't want to go. Why is it that they want you so badly?"

I flicked the reins and the carabao lurched forward.

"That's not much of a path," I told Marcel. "Would you really have left the cart with a friend and walked down this path? Where is the friend?"

"In his home at the other end of this path," Marcel said evenly, "this was truly the next step on our destination. If you can just trust me enough to step inside the tangle of the Forbidding, then you will see why. I realize you are not a girl who trusts easily, but you can't do everything on your own. Sometimes you have to trust that someone else has your interests in mind, too."

But I didn't trust him – not where the Forbidding was concerned. It was hard enough to trust family and friends to have your back there, never mind someone who you barely knew. I reached back to pat Osprey on the leg to try to tell him I was with him as much as I could be. Then I walked the carabao up to the edge of the tangle where the path seemed to roll up on itself like a curling fern leaf in spring. The edges of it formed waving tentacles. I hesitated at the edge, pulling on the reins to slow the carabao but there was a shout behind us. Tense, I looked back and saw the other carabao charging through the trees.

I needed to decide right now.

"It's real. And it's here. Come on, girl!" Marcel said in worried gasps. "Just go."

Osprey moaned.

I shook my head, trying to convince myself to go against every instinct and walk right into the tangles of the Forbidding. I was going to have to trust Marcel. I didn't want to, but what other chance was there?

I clenched my teeth, flicked the reins, and let the carabao step into the tangled mass. Tentacles reached toward us, waving and swaying and the path rolled upward like a wave, taking us with it and out of sight of the forest. We rolled sharply to the side and then I had the oddest feeling that the carabao was walking upside down – oh, its feet were still on the path, but the path was somehow in the sky.

I focused my eyes on a single point ahead and refused to look anywhere else. At this rate, I was going to be ill – and I couldn't afford to be ill. Everyone else was ill already.

The carabao couldn't manage more than a walk on a path that twisted like a corkscrew, so I held onto his reins with one hand and wrapped my other hand back to help balance Osprey who was slumped against my back. I gritted my teeth and hoped he could just hold on.

There were no more shouts behind us, no sound of pursuit, but the Forbidding tentacles wrapped toward us, waving and slicing at the air and I realized Marcel was right. This path was some kind of gap. If we kept to the path – though it tangled in strange ways – the tentacles couldn't reach us.

I bit my lip, focused now on keeping the carabao straight while a voice sang to me from the Forbidding.

YESSS LITTLE BEE. YOU HAVE RETURNED. LET US SSSSIFT YOU. LET USSS SEE YOUR HEART.

Somehow, I always ended up back here – in some secret heart of the Forbidding as it tried to fold me in and fold into me. I did not enjoy the process any more than I did the last time. I flinched from its mental touch. It seemed to almost glow when it touched the feather in my chest.

YOU ARE BOUND, TOO. SSSURPRISSING.

Great. Juste had even surprised the Forbidding. He'd surprised dark magic. He should be proud.

NOT DARK. FUNDAMENTAL.

Sure.

I tried to ignore it as it shuffled through my mind.

"How much further do we have to travel down this 'gap,' Marcel?" I asked.

No answer. I turned to look and saw he was slumped over Osprey just as Osprey was slumped into me. Both unconscious. Both in need of help. And I was leading them into oblivion. I swallowed down my curse. What was the point in cursing when you'd gone so far into insanity?

The sun was still setting. And it stayed like that – a thin band of red across the rim of the sky even as what felt like hours ticked by. I could have sworn we'd ridden for half the night – my mouth was certainly dry enough, my belly empty and my bladder in need of relief. But though it felt like hour upon hour, still that narrow band of sunset remained.

Ixtap had said that time in the Forbidding acted differently. And when I used the undertrails, things were certainly different. I'd traveled a great distance in the blink of an eye. This felt like that again, except that instead of experiencing the blink of the eye, I was experiencing everything that happened in between.

At least we weren't being hunted in here. I saw no Wings or their spirit-birds flashing above me. I heard no shouts or hooves. It was just me and the nervous carabao, my two unconscious friends, and the ever-rolling, ever bubbling Forbidding.

When the path turned a final time and we stepped into something new, I could hardly trust my own eyes. My mouth dropped open with surprise.

CHAPTER SIX

The path came out into a clearing where a river rushed over tumbled rocks cloaked in moss. A small bridge spanned the distance and on either side were buildings. My mind was listing them before I even asked it to. A waterwheel. A large well. A town square. What looked like an inn. Several freestanding homes. And tents everywhere like the festival had come to town. It was as if a village was just sitting here in the heart of the Forbidding. It was impossible to believe. And yet it was here.

The small patch of buildings and greenery was surrounded by Forbidding, dark and clawing, but there were areas where it had been freshly burned and others where the tentacles had been cleared back. Curious, I glanced behind my shoulder. The small path entered through an actual gap between two rocks. It felt almost too much like my own imagination. I shook my head to clear it.

Around the perimeter of the town were people. They faced the edge of the Forbidding, their mouths open and arms up. It was a moment before I realized that they were singing. The song lodged into my mind almost immediately and I couldn't shake the feeling that I was listening to the song even when I was well away from the singers.

The sunset splashed across the buildings as a bell began to ring and people tumbled out of them headed toward a long, low hall. Some moved to replace the singers joining in the song and shifting it slightly to a lower note. They looked like normal people. Men, women, and children – dressed in somewhat worn clothing, but they were like I'd expect at home. They even wore swords at their sides. That got my attention. Swords. And not a Claw to be seen. Was this a hidden village I'd never heard of? Perhaps they had been overlooked by Le Majest.

And then someone noticed me, pointing with a gasp. A large man disentangled himself from the crowd and hurried toward us but there were already others coming from either side. Men with weapons drawn and grim expressions. I drew my own sword. They wouldn't take Osprey from me without a fight. I glanced behind me, but some trick of the light made the path nearly impossible to see. I'd try negotiation, but if that failed, I'd have to go right back into the gap, whether I could see it or not.

I shifted in my seat, hands twitching as I tried to read their eyes and expressions, eyes darting to one and then the next and then …

Alect!

He trotted toward me with a huge smile on his face, waving frantically.

"Aella!" he called, his youthful face lighting up with excitement. He was holding a sword in one hand, sweating and huffing as if he'd been hacking at the Forbidding.

My heart stuttered in my chest.

I'd thought I'd never see him again. That maybe I'd die, or he would, or something else would happen that would bar us from each other forever. I fought back tears, as my smile widened. He was here. He was safe. I could hardly believe what I was seeing.

I couldn't get down from the back of the carabao – not

without dumping both Osprey and Marcel onto the ground, but I didn't have to. Alect was there in a flash, wrapping his arms around my waist in a rough hug and then talking a league a minute.

"Aella! You're here! I thought I'd never see you again! You wouldn't believe where we are. Did you have any idea there were actual outposts in the Forbidding? I didn't. They hold back the dark magic with singing. Singing! Can you believe it? You'd be terrible at it since you're such a bad singer. There's hundreds of people here and we drill every day while the older people plan. We're going to fight the Empire, Aella, and now you can fight with us and use whatever you learned. Even bees have to be good for something, right? And Retger got back last night. But I've hardly had a chance to talk to him. They keep him cooped up in the command room and when he's eating he's always talking to this pretty girl he brought with him or they're worrying over another sick man they brought to the healer. Oh! We have a real healer here. A Wing. Can you believe it? Her bird is an owl which doesn't feel much like healing to me, but she told me to shut my fool mouth when I said so."

My mouth must have been hanging open as he dropped back to the ground and gestured to the guards who were looking back and forth bemusedly.

"These are Francen and Chesma and they're on gap duty today. This is my sister, Aella! The one who was stolen. She's going to be a Wing."

"Maybe not anymore," I said, my eyes wide as I realized that dozens of people were gathering now. And they weren't harried and ragged like I'd expected. They were dressed in something that could be considered a uniform. Forest green wool jackets buttoned with a double row of steel buttons. No embroidery.

Breeches in a light fawn color. Their faces were hard and stern and while they smiled slightly at Alect, they watched me guardedly. Eyes flicked over my hands and neck as if they were looking for a tattoo. They wouldn't find one. Yet.

"Alect! I can't believe it's you," I said when I finally had a chance to cut in on his excitement. I grabbed his hands, gripping them as if I could hug just that part of him. I couldn't get down from the back of the carabao without letting Osprey or Marcel drop but I wanted to squeeze my brother and tell him what he meant to me. "Can we get my friends to a healer? It's so good to see you, but they're in bad shape."

"Of course, we can," he said, leading me after him. "You're going to love Sawet. She can heal anything."

I hoped he was right about that. I clutched Osprey and Marcel close as Alect led my carabao through the streets. Our escort stayed with us, hands on hilts, eyes on me. They saw me as a threat. If only I was as powerful as they thought I was, I'd make the Empire surrender all by myself.

"Is Raquella safe?" I asked when he glanced back at me.

Alect laughed. "Safe? She's the one that found this place! The Forbidding grabbed her, and she twisted around and found a gap. And then it was just a matter of finding some more. This place is so weird. We thought it took all day to find her but by the time we did, it had only been minutes. Same with all the people that are brought here. They're from so far away and it feels like it takes ages and ages to make the journey but the whole time the sun never moves. It's the folding. Time doesn't work the same way here that it does outside."

"I thought I saw her pulled into the Forbidding. I thought she was dead," I said, my head whirling with everything he was saying. I didn't even care about all the curious faces watching us. "She's fine?"

"Fine? She's doing great! She's a natural at healing. Sawet has her busy from dawn to dusk and way into the night every night. She's going to be a healer. But what do you mean you saw her?" he asked.

My bee arrived so suddenly that I didn't answer right away. He zipped through the crowd and buzzed around my head with the joy of reunion. And then another one and another one joined the first. They ringed me like a trio of happy moons, orbiting my every move.

"The bees have eyes," I said simply, and my brother's eyes grew wide as soup plates.

He shook his head and then pointed at a sign above us. "We're here! Let's get your friends inside."

The sign read "Sawet" and someone had carved a pair of sawet owls on either side of the name as if that was all that needed to be said.

I moved as if I was going to hop down from the carabao, but I stopped at the sound of swords being drawn from sheaths.

"That's my sister," Alect protested. Around him, at least a dozen women and men had their blades drawn and all eyes were on me.

"We know, boy," the one he'd named Francen said. He was thick in the arms and his dark hair was thinning. His eyes were hard as stone. "And we're happy that you were able to greet your sister, but the happy welcome ends here. She goes before the council or she goes into the brig."

"You can't do that!" Alect protested.

“Why do you have your swords drawn?” I asked warily.

“Put your blades on the ground, nice and easy,” the one named Chesma said, flicking her own blade toward me to remind me who was holding all the power. “By order of the council, you are under the custody of the Single Wing. Don’t move, or we’ll cut you down and leave your corpse for the ravens.”

CHAPTER SEVEN

I was now in the custody of the Single Wing.

I was wanted by everyone – the Single Wing, the Empire, Osprey, Juste. Everyone. Frustration bubbled up in me and in answer, my bees began to buzz. I almost called them out to join me. These guards would be thrown into utter chaos if I let them loose. And then we'd see who was under arrest and who was running for the tangles of Forbidding, screaming as bees stung them all over.

I drew a long breath. Running into battle without thinking first had gotten me in enough trouble already. This time, I needed to think. This time, I needed to take my time.

"Can you take care of these two, Alect?" I asked gently, offering my younger brother a half-smile. "I really hope we get to catch up soon. But you should know that I love you and I've missed you."

I slid carefully down from the carabao as Alect supported Osprey and Marcel. I gave him a hug the moment I was free.

"I missed you, too," he said, but he looked confused from me to the Single Wing guards. Which was the normal reaction to this kind of betrayal, but I was getting used to betrayal. "I'll take care of your friends."

"This is Marcel – he's traveled with us today and guided us

to this point. He had a head injury," I said, pointing to Marcel. "And this is Wing Osprey. He has a fever." No need to add that he had one of my bees inside him. "And they are both Single Wing and have the tattoos to prove it, so hopefully these over-eager achievers won't decide to arrest them, too."

I couldn't keep the bite out of my words, but I did put my swords back in my sheathes and I handed them to Alect. The Single Wing could decide what they wanted to do with that.

Alect was nodding. His hands holding Osprey and Marcel in place, but his eyes – crinkled with worry – were fixed on me and my new captors.

"I'll take care of them, Aella, and then I'll come find you," Alect said.

I offered him my bravest half-smile and then allowed the guards to push me forward, ahead of them. I waited until they had me out to the street again and away from the healers – waited until I'd lost sight of Alect. Tearing myself away from Osprey seemed to almost hurt. As much as I trusted my brother, would he really be able to find Osprey the help he needed? Would he keep him bound as I'd asked?

There was no way to know. I'd just have to trust that he could. But I was finding it harder and harder to trust other people. I was too used to being let down.

"Do you want to tell me what this is about?" I asked the nearest guard.

"I think we'll let the council tell you," she said, spitting at my feet. "If they let you live that long."

Something tightened inside me.

"You don't mean that."

"Don't we? Just last night we found a traitor here. He'd slipped information to the enemy that led to three of ours being slaughtered in Karkatua. We hung him in a Forbidding tangle and let nature do its ugly work. We'll do the same to you, if it's proven that you're a traitor. And we think you are."

Around us, the haunting singing of those holding back the Forbidding mixed with her sour words. Who would have thought that song would work? And how did it work? But that was a question for another time.

"I have never betrayed the Single Wing," I said.

"And anyone who was with you will be held equally culpable," she said.

I shivered. They were accusing me falsely. And they'd seemed pretty unreasonable about that so far. And now they planned to take out their wrath on Osprey and Marcel as well. I gritted my teeth together and tried to keep my frustrations in check.

We had nearly arrived at a very busy building. Messenger boys flew in and out the front door, letting heat and tempers flare out the door behind them. It was set in front of a square, and in the square, soldiers were drilling. They were positioned in two-man teams and as one team attacked with long poles, the other team practiced a coordinated defense that pulled the enemy from his horse while seeing to it that each partner remained safe from the stomping feet or charge of the enemy. I watched in wonder until the guards pulled me along.

"We'll never get far watching other people work," one of them said.

"Who is doing the military training?" I asked.

The woman grunted, but she couldn't seem to stop herself

from answering smugly, “We have former Claws in our ranks, as well as original colonists. People who know everything there is to know about fighting with or for the Empire.”

They pulled me through the courtyard and to the large building, past a pair of stationed guards outside the entrance and a scribe hurriedly scribbling and tying little messages to the feet of pigeons before setting them loose into the dusk. I wondered if time folded for them, too, or if the Forbidding only affected those on the ground. If Osprey was well, he could find out for us.

The door opened to a wall of sound – shouting voices and the clink of metal on metal. All I could see was a hallway with three half-opened doors.

Chesma dropped my arm, nodding to Francen. She hurried into one of the lit rooms and the sound grew louder and then quieter again as she stepped in, closing the door behind her. I tried to peer into the half-opened doorway, but Francen tugged me into a room on the other side of the corridor.

“What is this?” I asked as he shut the door behind me. This room was set up like a small study with a study desk, two mismatched chairs. Parchment and ink were ready on the desk. It was meager and not at all luxurious, but there was something familiar about the collapsible bird perch in one corner.

“Shhh, now,” Francen said and I didn’t like the gleam in his eye. I tried to shake his grip from my arm.

“I want to see my brother,” I said boldly. “Retger of House Shrike. Or anyone else from my House.”

He paused, looking worried for a heartbeat, but he shook his head and leaned in. I flinched from the look in his eye. I didn’t like what it suggested.

"You don't make the demands here, High'un. We do."

"I'm no High'un," I said, trying to stay calm. Why was he treating me like an enemy? "Where's Wing Ivo? Alect said he was here."

"It's not Wing Ivo you'll be talking to," he said, his gaze threatening.

I tried to take another step back, but he kept his grip on my arm and now I was getting worried. Why had he brought me to an empty room instead of to see this council he'd talked about? Why was he threatening me with hints?

"In a moment, someone important is going to come in here and talk to you," he said evenly, shooting a furtive glance to the door. "And then I'm sure the council will have their mock court and they'll sentence you as they please. But before they do, I want answers of my own. My sister's in Glorious Ingvar. I need to know how to get her out of that place safely. So, tell me. How did you get out of the city?"

"I can't help you," I said.

His grip tightened and his other hand raised, a knife gleaming in it. "I'm serious. I'm a desperate man. I wouldn't usually do this, but when they get you in there, they won't have time to get the information I need. I need a dependable way into the city, and I need it tonight, so tell me, girl, how did you get out?"

"I flew over the wall," I said through clenched teeth.

I didn't see the butt end of the dagger coming until it smashed me in the jaw. Pain flared through my face. I bit back a scream. It was all I could do to hold it back, but my bees erupted from me, surrounding him and shoving him back. I clenched my jaw and yanked my hand out from his grip.

He shrieked and at the same moment, the door crashed open and a spirit-bird flared violently toward me, its wings flapping aggressively. It snapped up a cluster of bees in its owl beak and dove for more. I flinched as it swallowed up my bees and flinched again. It was physically painful when they disappeared.

"To me," I whispered to them. I held out my hands, absorbing my bees as quickly as they could return.

The owl flapped in front of me – there but not there – and then vanished with the last of my bees.

"It was sensible for you to quiet those abominations," a crystal-clear voice said. "They're horrific to look at and useless for anything of value."

The door shut behind her with a snick and I gasped as my eyes met those of Wing Essena.

"I thought you were dead," I said in barely a whisper.

"I'd hoped you were," she replied, her lips thinning as she pressed them together so hard that she could have crushed rocks between them. "And yet here you are. And a blushing bride, I hear. Congratulations."

"How can you know that?" I asked, my heart thundering so hard that I couldn't get it under control. There were no windows in the room, and she stood before the only door, her guard beside her, his eyes flicking from her to me and back. Two against one.

"Didn't you see the pigeons outside? Where there are pigeons, you know that Xectare and I are not far away."

She watched me, clearly waiting for a reaction, so I refused to give her one. Xectare. Of course. They were still working together.

"It can be hard to find your way into a revolution," Essana said calmly. "Sometimes it helps if they find you surrounded by corpses and half-dead yourself. It helps even more if you tell the story of how you desperately tried to save one of their own. Too bad Wing Osprey stole you away for Le Majest before I could free you."

She looked at me with big, innocent eyes and I had to swallow down bile. I could tell from how she said it that they'd believed her. Even the members of my family must have.

"It's handy that you brought him here with you. That sells the story even better. Brave Aella who caught her captor. Too bad it wasn't until after you were turned against us. Too bad it's just a ruse to get you on our side."

"What are you talking about?" I felt ill.

"I'm just telling you the story first. There's no point in denying it. All the details add up. And if you don't go along with it, I'll kill Wing Ivo. I've been tasked with tending him in his ill state … and he needs so many herbs that no one would even blink at me offering him more.

"No one will believe you."

"I think they will. Especially since you're married to our enemy now.

She sidled around the desk, staring me down.

"What do you want?" I made my voice as firm as I could. My face still hurt but that pain warred with my sudden fears for Alect and Osprey out there in the camp. None of them were safe while Essena had the ear of the people in charge.

"You're going to be silent when I bring you in there. Not a word of protest when I tell them of your crimes. You'll admit that you married Le Majest and then you'll not say a word when they ask you if the rest is true. You'll look at your boots and accept what comes next."

"Or you'll kill Ivo," I said grimly.

"Among other people. If you find he's not motivation enough, then maybe I'll kill Osprey, too. Still not enough? I can tell by your face that you're going to be difficult, but I'm not worried, Aella. Do you know why? That precious family of yours is here and I know how much you love your family. You'd die to keep them safe – in fact, you likely will die while keeping them safe."

"I thought you were the nice one," I said through gritted teeth.

"I am," she said simply. "Do you understand the bargain?"

"Yes," I said, but understanding a thing was not the same as agreeing to it.

There was a knock on the door.

"Let's go see the Single Wing Council," Essena said boldly, signaling for me to go ahead of her.

CHAPTER EIGHT

It was Francen who led us across the hall and into the noisy room beyond. I'd expected an inn common room. What I saw took my breath away.

A long table was laid across the entire room with long benches on either side and behind each person seated on the bench were a cluster of others. Across the surface of the table, maps, candles, small tokens, and lists with quill and ink were spread almost haphazardly. It only took a glance to confirm that these were maps of the Far Stones and lists of required items for the Single Wing. The one nearest me listed food supplies and the quantities along with the final sum along the column were enough to make my stomach do flips.

The people seated, arguing, around the benches were clearly leaders of the Single Wing. There were more than a dozen, grim-looking men and women, some grizzled, some fresh. Some whole and some with grievous wounds. Together, they looked up from their disagreement at the entry of Wing Essena.

Wing Essena cleared her throat, her pale owl popping into existence and perching on her shoulder – a mark of her authority. The arguments and murmurs began to fade out she spoke over the last hurried conversations. And as she spoke, my eyes roved along the edge of the waiting people. The man nearest me had his coat cut in the way of the eastern miners, another – a silkie fisherman – still was wearing his fishing rig. The next had a face I could have sworn I recognized. And the next …

Abghar stood up so suddenly that his bench nearly toppled. The look on his face was relief tinged with joy – I knew that because I felt the same way myself and felt it even more strongly as my eyes – noting that he was strong even if he was worn and gaunt – strayed behind him to glance at my brothers and sisters waiting patiently there.

My breath caught, tears welling up so suddenly that I couldn't blink them back. When I'd seen Alect I knew there would be more of them here but seeing my family right in front of me was almost too much joy to bear.

Helissa's eyes lit with happiness and Oska dropped something he was holding – a tin mug? – with a clatter. I could hardly even distinguish the other faces now through my fast-flowing tears. I thought that maybe Helissa was striding toward me, but I could barely see a thing.

Joy – powerful and rich – bowled me over more intensely than if I'd been knocked off my feet. I thought I might never see them again. I thought that some might be dead before I ever could and now here they were within inches of me being able to touch them.

I took an involuntary step forward.

Wing Essena stepped between us with a piercing shout of, "Hold! Hold, all of you! Someone keep House Shrike back."

"What's the meaning of this?" Aghar bellowed and still, I was blinking too many tears away to see.

"This child is a traitor to the Far Stones and the Single Wing. You all know this by the report I delivered to you this morning. She has been wed to Le Majest of the Winged Empire and he is hotly in pursuit of her. Just having her here endangers us all – but worse yet, she is his wife and bound to him. Whether she has family here or not, she is our enemy now by bond and blood."

"You're mad if you think – " that was Anfrea – always so protective. I blinked away tears as Wing Essena spoke over her and I barely even heard the Wing as I drank in their faces – most of them had their eyes on me, ignoring the Wing and I saw the sympathy and worry and deep delight echoed in every face and shared with me. Oh, it was good to be home with them – even if we weren't home at all. Home was where they were, and I was here with them. Home, home, home. My bees buzzed in happy sympathy.

And then I heard what Essena was saying, "… which is why we can't allow the feelings of one family to damage what we are here to achieve. This is for all the Far Stones. This is for all our families and all our hopes and dreams. We must not allow a traitor – a spy! – here in our midst."

"You can't even know that the rumors you heard are true," Helissa said, her voice trembling like she was trying so hard to keep calm. And my heart leapt at the expressions on all my siblings' faces – they'd all morphed into something I recognized from my own mirror. Their mouths were firm lines. Their eyes burned. Stray curls sprang out from their hair, as if even those curls were desperate to put distance between themselves and all that fury.

"And yet I do know," Wing Essena said. "And I can prove it."

She tugged my shirt open so suddenly that I couldn't stop her. I gasped as the single feather – glowing moonlight silver – showed through my skin.

There was a gasp from around the room and I saw enough

to realize that every other face around that table had a look on it somewhere close to terror. If that frightened them, then I supposed they should be glad they didn't know more. The truth of what they were up against was a lot worse than a teenage girl with a glowing feather in her chest.

But my siblings – oh my siblings – their faces never changed. What did change was the sound of steel drawing from their blades. They were all there – Abghar, Oska, Anfrea, Adigale, Helissa, Raquella – Royn and Fawren, my brothers-in-law – Gressa my sister-in-law. But not Awet or Retger and Zayana, thank the stars and skies, and not the children. Because House Shrike only drew steel for a reason and now blades drew all around the table – blades pointed at my family.

"There's no need for violence here," Wing Essena said placidly, as if she hadn't started all of this. "No need to fight family against family. We need every sword we can muster. We can't afford to spare any on squabbles. Not when the traitor will go quietly. And she's agreed to do that, haven't you girl? We'll walk her to the edge of camp and let her make her way through the Forbidding. For the Forbidding gives and the Forbidding takes away and all justice is served eventually."

"Don't do it," Abghar said. "Don't let her cow you, sister. We are House Shrike."

"We are relentless," Raquella said from behind him, her sword tip wavering with nerves as she found her place defending her brother's back. They were forming a porcupine – a tried and true formation for fighting the Forbidding. I'd been in one before when things were particularly grim and every hand needed to hold a blade.

"We can't afford a traitor here," a bluff man from the other side of the table said, head shaking sadly as if he felt bad for what he was suggesting. Around him, others agreed with similar sober nods.

"Aye, Chandres, we can't allow a traitor. We must trust Wing Essena."

"Stand down, House Shrike. We bid you remain calm," Chandres – the bluff man – reiterated.

"Don't spill their blood needlessly, girl," Wing Essena warned. "You know you deserve what comes next. Don't jeopardize your family with your lies."

And maybe I would have been cowed a few months ago. But I was watching my siblings' hard faces and I knew something now – I knew I couldn't protect them if I bowed to evil people. I knew that sometimes accepting the lesser of two evils was still accepting an evil. They were willing to risk everything to stand with me. I wouldn't take that from them.

I felt the bees buzzing in me, building their power – but this time it was not a wild, angered buzzing – it was a buzzing made of righteous fury – the need to set things right.

"If we're going to talk about traitors," I said, "then you'd better stop threatening my family, Wing Essena."

Her eyes narrowed. "Think twice before accusing me, girl."

"I have thought twice. I've thought three times," I said boldly, projecting my voice through the room. "I've thought about how you threatened to kill people in this room if I didn't remain silent. I've thought about how you threatened my family." At that, the porcupine made a careful step toward me as my siblings moved to get nearer to Wing Essena and me. "I've thought about how you think these people will believe you and not me. But why would they do that? You've worked for the Winged Empire since before you received that owl, and you'll keep on working for them. You stole me from my people and helped Le Majest keep me confined. When we were beset by the Forbidding, you left your apprentice to die and tried to save yourself. And when I arrived here – finally reuniting with my family and bringing to them information and knowledge they can use against the Empire and against the Forbidding, you try to threaten my life. I think they'll believe me. I think they'll hear my heart – that I long to see our continent free and our people bold and prosperous. I think that when they consider it, they'll realize you've never really been on their side."

"Are you about done?" she asked calmly.

"Not even close."

"Do you mean to tell us all that you aren't married to Le Majest?" she said with a glimmer of triumph in her eye.

"I am married to Le Majest," I said and a gasp went up from the whole room. But my family made my heart roar. They completed their circuit to me, surrounding me and edging Wing Essena aside.

"Don't do this," she told them calmly. "There's no need to kill all of you. Only your sister has betrayed us."

"She's betrayed nothing," Abghar said, standing between us with his sword drawn. "As the head of House Shrike, I say that we stand with our sister."

"We do," Oska and Adigale said together from behind him.

"Who took her blades, Wing? If that was you, you'll return them or pay dearly," Helissa could be very insightful when she wanted to be.

"She had no blades," Essena said.

"Her man Francen tried to take them from me – mine and Wing Osprey's. I gave them to Alect instead, but it was Francen who gave me this swollen jaw," I said. Because I was done with secrets and protecting the guilty.

There was a shift from the room around us – they were nervous now – not certain who to believe.

"If you're really with us," Chandres said, "then why have you married Le Majest?"

"It was a marriage in absentia." I tried to match his calm, but my bees were raging. "I had no more say in it than you do. And I want it no more than you do."

"Lies," Wing Essena stated just as calmly. "All lies. We all know that the Skybinders don't work like this. She's a clever trap meant to distract us and turn one of our strongest families from us."

But she was showing her true colors. Her bird slipped from her grasp, sailing into the sky. He blinked his white owlish blink, but he was diminished, smaller than normal.

"You're the one who taught me the power of words, Essena," I said, careful to leave off her title. "Your lies have diminished your bird and shrunk your power. And no wonder when you are feeding it hate and paranoia rather than the truth. If anyone needs proof, I'd be willing to bet it's in the messages you send with your pigeons. Have you been informing on your new friends, Wing?"

Chandres' jaw clenched tightly, and he looked from Wing Essena to me and back.

"Regardless of what anyone else believes," Abghar said loudly for the room to hear, "this is our sister. As head of House Shrike,

I say she is welcome with us. We'll be in our camp deciding what outcome this will have on our alliances and choices for the future. You'd all do well to consider the same." He turned but then paused. "Oh, and Wing Essena? I believe my little sister. If you're still in the camp by dawn it will be blood feud between yours and mine."

"What does that mean?" Wing Essena asked, shaken. Maybe there weren't blood feuds across the sea.

"It means any one of us who sees you will kill you on sight."

"I'm not so easy to kill," she said coolly.

"Aren't you?" Abghar asked. And the quiet threat of his words shot a spike of fear through me. Thank the skies and stars that he was on my side.

We marched together from the room and as soon as we were through the door I could hardly stand. A huge hug from Oska swept me off my feet and then Abghar was there roughing up my hair and Royn was nodding in a friendly manner and Raquella was trying to kiss both my cheeks at once while Helissa scolded us all.

"Hurry, hurry!" she chided. "We need to get to the house and see to the children before that wretched Wing decides to make good on her threats."

I could hardly breathe as they swept me through the encampment or village or whatever it was. I kept catching glimpses of men and women training with weapons or fletching arrows or sharpening blades and all of that was in between glances of my family's happy faces.

"We missed you, Shrikeling," Adigale said, kissing my head like mother used to, and then Oska leaned in with a worried frown.

"Retger told us about Father. It shouldn't have been you who had to be there for that."

"We all wish we could have held your hands," Raquella said, tears brimming in her eyes. "Oh, Aella, you wouldn't believe the things we've seen. We had to flee into the Forbidding, and we found these crazy places."

She pointed to the nearest building as if that could explain the strangeness of a village plopped right in the middle of the Forbidding with a twisting path leading to it.

"It's a place to gather and strategize," Oska added. "And now that you're here, we're all safe and ready to finish readying the plan. We strike in a week. We'll take Karkatua. It's weakened already by the attack of those strange barbarians."

"The Hissan," I said. "And I could have sworn I saw you there."

"You did!" He said cheerfully. "Or at least, you could have. I was there, talking to the Single Wing in the city."

"But how did you get here?" I asked, stunned.

"That's how it works, silly," Raquella laughed, dragging me toward a noisy well-lit house. "Time doesn't mean the same thing inside the Folding."

"Wait!" I protested. "I can't go in there. Alect took Marcel and Osprey to the healer and they'll be in danger from Essena."

Abghar paused, looking at me before nodding briskly. "Everyone inside except Oska and Raquella. We four will go retrieve Awet and Aella's friend from the healers. The rest of you set up a perimeter and for skies sakes make some kind of supper.

Conflict with supposed 'allies' makes me hungry as a Forbidding-bear."

My eyes grew wide as he spoke but my siblings hurried to obey in a way I would never have guessed – none of us had ever been particularly submissive. Raquella, Oska, and I hurried to follow him as he trotted toward the house of healing.

"It's unlikely to go south, though they might talk about it for a while. We're a strong house here. Maybe not as strong as a Wing, but strong all the same. They will decide to back us. And we always back our own, Shrikeling."

"Thank you, Abghar," I said gratefully. "And umm. I think I should confess something."

He shot me a worried look.

"Not something bad exactly." I was suddenly feeling very nervous.

"Just say it!" Raquella said, impatient.

"The man – Osprey – that we're going to go get. He's a Wing, too."

"We should also take Ivo with us," Abghar said, thinking aloud. "Retger feels strongly about keeping him safe. What if Wing Essena wasn't bluffing? We don't want him dead, either."

I was nodding gratefully before he finished. "And Osprey is also my prisoner."

"Grabbed one of them?" Abghar asked. "That's gutsy, sister."

"Thank you," I said, feeling my cheeks heat. "He's the Wing who came to our house that first night with Le Majest."

Abghar froze, nearly stumbling over his own feet he stopped

so quickly.

"Perhaps we could trade him to Wing Essena for a little peace," he said. "After all, she's bent and determined to root the magic out. Maybe she can get it out of him."

"He's under my protection," I said repressively. "I want that to be clear."

"Retger said it's rather more than that," Raquella said with a smirk that only made Abghar's face darker. "He said he'd left you with a strong young Wing who was looking at you like he might weave you a bridal wreath then and there."

Abghar swiveled to her. "Retger didn't share that with me."

"We can't tell you everything, Abghar. Not when you get so upset."

We were crossing the road toward the building I'd first seen when we arrived – the healers. Another group of people was making their way there from the direction of the Council hall. I stiffened and quickened my pace.

"Stop teasing him, Raquella," Oska said with quiet authority. "We need to pick up the pace. Besides, it sounds like Aella is married to someone else – whether she likes it or not – and we'll have to dispatch this new husband for the sake of our sister's honor before anyone marries anyone else."

That quieted us all and we quickened our pace like he ordered. My heart pounded in my chest. It felt good to have someone else care about my problems like they were their own. But at the same time, it felt terrible to think that I was dragging them into this, too. Just being with them was like salve to the soul. The thought of them being hurt or dying because of me … my heart shied away from the thought.

We skirted around a group of archers firing volleys on command. They were fast, quickly drawing the next arrow from the quiver and firing the next shaft by the time the order was given.

"Draw. Aim. Loose. Draw. Aim. Loose," the drill instructor chanted, his eyes on us and on the other hurrying group, but the long poplar branch he held in his hand tapped the shoulder of any archer who allowed himself to be distracted by us.

We were past them and nearing a ring where someone was patiently teaching porcupine fighting techniques to two groups of twenty people. He had them in the porcupine but teaching a group to move like that and fight together wasn't easy and as I watched one group stumbled and barely avoided cutting themselves on their own swords. They'd need a lot of practice to get that right. My family had years behind us.

All around me, people hustled to work or to train, to move supplies, to cook food – I could smell that! – to ready themselves for the coming conflict. But even what must be a few hundred people couldn't be enough. When we had Osprey and Ivo secure, then I'd ask my siblings more. Was there a plan? Was it a good one? I felt tense just asking myself those questions. Our futures and lives hung on the answers to those questions.

We reached the House of Healing before the other group and I hurried in the door before any of my siblings could, past the squeak of the little woman by the door who was hanging up healing herbs, past the woman whose scolding words told me to slow down and stop.

"Would you slow her, Raquella Shrike? She should not be disturbing the patients. Or have you brought me a lunatic to cure?"

"No Mother Sawet, she's my sister," Raquella laughed. "But there's been a big scuffle at the Council Hall and my sister claims that Wing Ivo's life is threatened and that of Wing Osprey, too, so we've come to bring them to our house to keep them safe."

"Nonsense! They're best kept here."

I had already looked in every door on this floor and was sprinting up the steps. Mother Sawet could protest all she wanted, but I didn't trust Essena. I didn't trust her bird not to fly in here and smother one of those two before I even found them.

"Hurry, Raquella," Abghar barked. "We'll hold the doors."

I cleared the last step and peeked in the first door in the white-washed corridor. An empty bed. The next one – empty.

I turned back into the hall and nearly bumped into a white-faced Alect.

"What's happening?" he asked.

"There's been a fight. The family decided to stand with me and Wing Essena doesn't like it."

His face went from surprise to grim determination in an instant. "We need to get out of here. The House of Healing is no place for a fight."

I nodded. "We're here to get Wing Ivo and Wing Osprey, too. Do you know where they are?"

He was already pulling me down the corridor to a large room at the end. We rushed through the door and Retger stepped back from an open window on the far side of the room, shaking his head.

"Fools! We had a plan and fighting amongst ourselves is not

it."

Our eyes met across the room and relief filled his.

"I didn't like leaving you back there," he said shortly. "Don't put me in that position again." He didn't wait for my nod before he was hurrying to one of the beds. "Can you stand, old man? I've grown too fond of you to let an over-stuffed owl snatch you away."

Wing Ivo coughed – deep and harsh – the kind of cough that sent a shiver of fear through me, but I didn't wait to watch Retger helping him up. My eyes were searching across the room. Beds lined the walls with basins and chairs beside them – clearly a room to keep the people who needed constant watch. I caught Zayana's eye and waved as she hurried to help Retger from the corner of the room she'd been in and she shook her head as if to ask what new disaster I'd brought with me.

And there! There he was. I didn't realize how tense I was until my bees quieted at the sight of him. He was bound and blindfolded still, and someone had cleaned his face and hands for him.

I rushed to his side, reaching my hand into his shirt to feel where my bee was at work. I felt it buzz against my hand through his skin and I had the strangest feeling that I knew what it was doing. It was still slowly untangling the feather bit by bit from the Forbidding at Osprey's core, burning out each tendril one by one.

I pushed his sweat-soaked hair back, wishing I could see his eyes. "Osprey? Can you hear me?"

His breathing was even and there was no response. Maybe the healer had given him something.

Behind me, Raquella whistled. "Maybe I'll wander off to the court of Le Majest if it means bringing back captives like that one."

"It also means having them hunt you down and try to kill you, Raquella," Retger said gruffly. "Come and help Zayana support Wing Ivo. She can't do it alone and you two girls aren't strong enough to carry the hunter."

He joined me beside Osprey's bed.

"We'll carry him but he's going to be heavy. I'll take his shoulders and you grab him around the knees."

"I'm glad you made it here safely," I said, wide-eyed. "I didn't even know this place existed."

"Neither did I," he grunted. "But I found a Single Wing safe house and sent everyone I could to find you and they directed me here. It turns out that they know Wing Ivo and every Wing we can turn to the cause is valuable. Even this one, if he can be turned."

"I told you before that he's Single Wing," I said, grunting as I lifted Osprey's legs.

"And I told you that I don't like the way you look at each other. It's going to be trouble."

We followed Zayana and Raquella down the stairs. Raquella looked over her shoulder to waggle her eyebrows at me. She was going to give me an earful by the time we found somewhere safe, I just knew it.

"Like you and Zayana?" I needled.

"Leave Zay out of it. She's far from home and she needs allies who can keep her safe from the Empire and the Forbidding.

Allies like House Shrike."

"Are you planning to deepen your alliance?" I teased in a low enough voice that Zayana wouldn't hear me.

He scowled and I smirked, but the humor was short-lived.

We reached the bottom of the stairs and found Oska and Abghar with weapons drawn before a knot of other rebels.

"We haven't decided and that's the point. You can't take all the Wings except for Wings Essena and Sawet to your house, Shrike," Chandres was saying. "We at House Pelican demand equal footing with House Shrike."

Abghar made an exasperated sound through his teeth. "This isn't about standing, Chandres. It's about defending our own. We were supposed to all want the same thing. We're supposed to be close to action. We have spies in every Far Stones city. As of yesterday, we have supplies in place, and marauding units in place, and havens within the Forbidding in place for strikes on Astar Harbor, Trakar, Karkatua, Far Port, and Portua Town. We're ready. The only thing that can stop us now isn't the Empire and it isn't the Forbidding, it's internal strife. And who is sowing that right now at the very cusp of our triumph? It's Wing Essena. She's created a conflict by accusing one of my House of treachery and demanding her death. Imagine if it was someone in your house, Chandres? Imagine if it was Eflan or Hiegar? What would you do? You'd do what I'm doing. You'd put them somewhere safe until cooler tempers brought wisdom. We're not going anywhere except our assigned house. I suggest you do the same. Go and let your head cool and we'll talk tomorrow morning."

"And Wing Essena?" Chandres asked coldly.

"Take her with you, by all means. I'd prefer she was watched since she's such a threat, and I'd prefer those pigeons were taken away and those two friends of hers – Francen and Chesma were watched, but there isn't much I can do about that. I can only guard my own and stay true to the course. Please tell me your House will do the same."

There were murmurs around Chandres and I realized that the men and women there weren't all from his house. Was that Ames in his ranks? The blacksmith who had turned Single Wing in Karkatua? It was hard to see past the guarding bodies of Oska and Abghar.

"We'll think on it House Shrike," Chandres said, but despite his reluctance, the murmurs around him seemed to favor Abghar, and more than one person – including Ames – made the sign of the bird to him before hurrying off.

Beside me, the healer was slinging a pouch over my neck.

"If you really must take him then you give him a spoon of these herbs in hot water four times a day and the salve for the wounds to stave off infection. Some of these are going very bad from neglect and I'd like to wring the neck of his traveling companions for allowing it to get so far."

She gave me a meaningful look – she must know I was traveling with him – and then she disappeared.

"Can we go?" Alect whispered.

"One more minute," Abghar cautioned. "Let them watch our united front for one more moment before we move. They must have it impressed on their minds. How tonight plays out will affect the success of the entire revolution. Either they listen, and reason and hope prevail, or they do not, and all is lost."

His words made us all feel sober as we waited until he made the sign of the bird and then led up across the darkening encampment to the house. Around us, the busy preparations were being put away for the day and the scent of food and tea was in the air, but in my heart, there blew a lonely wind of worry and loss. I caused trouble everywhere I went, even here with my family. And that just wasn't acceptable. There had to be a better way, if only I could find it.

Elsewhere in the Winged Empire

"General Petren?" the voice speaking to him was tentative. He'd never liked that about the Canaht orphans. No backbone to them. Not like his boy. His Vasyklo.

He turned, his eyes glaring into the boy and he backed up a step. Nineteen years old. Same age as his Vasyklo. The boy had been twelve – the oldest of the children taken – when he'd rounded them up and torn them from their parents. Even now, he remembered the faces of those pathetic fools whenever he looked at these grown children. The youngest of them was seven now. He was at the front of the ship looking out over the sea with a fake spyglass made from a roll of parchment.

Vasyklo would have liked that. Petren could barely stomach the softness of it.

And yet here he was, vanishing into the horizon with the hostages he'd taken seven years ago. Not to use them against their parents – but to save his son from having them used against him by yet another enemy. Or at least, he assumed that was why the boy had asked him to save them.

He should have said no.

He should have left on his own as his emperor had bid him.

But in leaving, he'd left his men, left his post, left his life.

He'd lost his home seven years ago to the whims of the

Emperor.

Lost his wife to those same whims thirteen years before that.

He wasn't ready to lose his son. Not even if it meant obeying his mad request and filling a ship full of orphans he cared nothing for to set sail for a continent he hated. Ah, Far Stones. There'd been bloodshed there and so much of it.

He realized suddenly that he was still staring at the boy. "What do you want?"

"Your dinner has been prepared below, sir."

He nodded grimly.

"If it's not too bold, sir," the boy continued, his face growing flushed with fear. And yet he was still speaking. "May we know now where you are taking us?"

"To fight a war, boy," Petren said. He knew in his bones he was right. His son had told him to leave – but where would he go except to join the one person he still cared something for?

BOOK TWO

Times of the heart turn and change,

Moons and seasons, for they range,

Times of laughter, times of grief,

Times when violent fear is chief,

Times of joy and of success,

Times when sorrow gives no rest,

So, harbor here with me, my friend,

Until your times come to an end.

- Songs of the Far Stones

CHAPTER NINE

The house my family had taken over was an ordinary house – just three rooms upstairs and three downstairs and an outhouse around the back, but it felt like something special when I finally walked through the doors. It wasn't just the smell of Anfrea's cooking – a smell that had home in it right to the bones – or the leaping children rushing to hug me and calling back and forth.

"Auntie Aella, look, I lost a tooth!"

"Auntie Aella, the baby can crawl now!"

"Auntie Aella, daddy said we had to fight to get you back. Did we win?"

"Watch me, watch me!"

It wasn't just the steady stream of hugs and kisses or the warmth I felt from constant smiles, constant catching of the eyes with someone else and a knowing look shared. No, it was more than that.

It was the safety of my brothers watching from both doors and guarding our house. It was the way they drew Ivo and Zayana in, setting them by the fire so Helissa could scold Retger on not bringing Zayana to them sooner and Adigale could tell her that she'd make a fine Far Reach bride – to her utter horror. Her bird flickered on her shoulder and off again so many times that I was sure it was a sign that she wished she could fly away, too, but her cat's eyes narrowed whenever she looked at Retger and she didn't try to leave or tell them she wasn't going to be a bride – which left me shocked and staring.

"Put him on my pallet," Raquella had demanded as soon as we cleared the door. Retger helped me put Osprey there – on a pallet in the corner of the main room. I didn't leave his side, and no one tried to make me. From the edge of that pallet, I watched them all – watched the teasing and laughing, the loving and the constant glances to me like a thousand touches to make sure I was still there.

"Aella!" my sister Adigale exclaimed when she caught sight of me. "You're injured. Your face is badly bruised and look at your hand. It's burned! Take that jacket off."

I took my jacket off, blushing as she fussed over me. "I'm not badly hurt."

"Not badly … Aella you have blood seeping through your shirt. Are you injured in other places?" She was already trying to look up the sleeve of my shirt.

"Can we at least do this somewhere private?" I squeaked.

"Raquella, gather some bandges and water," Adigale ordered. "Aella, you come with me."

She marched me to one of the front rooms – a cramped little spot covered in pallets. Clothing hung on rope lines along one wall. This was clearly where her little family was staying. One of her toddlers – Gessa – was fast asleep in the corner.

"Take off that shirt," she ordered. I stripped down and she gasped. "Aella."

"None of the injuries are serious," I assured her.

"The stitches in this one need to come out," she said, examining a wound Zayana had stitched for me. "And this one could have used stitches but now it's too late and it's just going to heal like that."

She ran a gentle finger beside the slash in my arm, clicking her tongue.

Raquella joined us, closing the door behind her. When she saw me, she clicked her tongue, too.

"Good thing I'm training to be a healer," she said wryly. "Aella might need me full-time."

"Take off the trousers, too," Adigale ordered. "I bet there are more injuries under there. You are a woman, Aella, not a Forbidding bear. You can't just scatter and coalesce again if you're too wounded. You need to take care of yourself."

They set to washing and bandaging my wounds and my hands until they finally agreed I could dress again.

"Try, try, try to take care of yourself," Adigale said, shaking her head as I finished buttoning my shirt. There was no censure in those eyes. All I saw was love.

I sucked in a long, hiccupping breath. It was like it hit me all at once. I was surrounded by people I loved and who loved me. Raquella's sudden hug knocked a little sob out of me and then Adigale wrapped us both up in her arms.

"Oh, my sisters, what will I do with you? You both worry me too much," she said. "I wish I could wrap you up in my arms and keep you here forever."

"Then who would take care of your children?" I laughed through my tears.

"I would," she said firmly. "I'm far more capable than you think. I can take care of everyone."

Our laughter woke little Gessa, and she waved us out of the room as she hurried to her daughter's side.

I followed Raquella out of the little room and made my way back to Osprey's side.

Raquella made tea and brought me some and as the night grew and dinner was served in small wooden bowls and children were put to bed and mothers and fathers grew busy with the business of settling them down and cleaning up, Raquella drifted to sit with me. We sat side by side, perched on the edge of Osprey's pallet and we sipped our tea in a quiet harmony.

"I've missed you," I said, arranging my short sword and Osprey's beside the pallet. Alect had brought them back with him. "I was worried that you wouldn't survive the journey."

"You were worried?" she teased. "I wouldn't think you had time with this one to moon over."

I jabbed her with my elbow – but lightly so she wouldn't spill her tea.

"It's complicated," I said.

"There's nothing complicated about falling in love," Raquella said breezily.

I scoffed and she raised her eyebrows as I explained. "I suppose it depends on who you fall in love with."

"He looks just fine to me," she said. "Long and lean with warm brown skin, rippling muscles, well-defined features, and a shadowed jaw? Yeah, you have it rough. He even smells nice. Is that pine? Also, does he have a brother?"

"Unfortunately, yes. It turns out I'm married to the brother. Against my will."

Her eyebrows rose and then she smirked, "Then maybe I'll take this one."

"No," my voice came out as a growl.

"See?" Raquella said sweetly. "Not complicated at all. Let me help you tend his injuries."

We unwrapped Osprey's bandages and his breathing hardly even hitched as we applied salve and new bandages. I tried not to blush at Raquella's approving looks as she worked over Osprey. Really, she didn't need to admire him so openly. I was desperate to change the subject to anything else.

"Is it true that the Single Wing is ready to launch a strike?"

She nodded and whispered as she worked. "Simultaneous strikes on every city in Far Stones. We start by burning any ships in the harbors. Burning barracks and guardhouses is second. Seizing the governor's house in Karkatua and the Grand Claw's house in Astar Harbor are also on our list. We were planning to strike tomorrow."

"So soon?" I whispered back, shocked. "How can you even get everywhere in time?"

She laughed. "This single encampment isn't everyone. This was the one that was supposed to strike Glorious Ingvar, but that won't work now that the people there rebelled on their own. We lost our supplies and our contacts in the chaos. We don't have time to get them back – or access. We received word this morning that Le Majest has declared martial law on the whole continent and a sunset curfew enforced by Claws. Reinforcements from the mainland arrived in Glorious Ingvar this morning. Their ships must have sailed by magic to get here so quickly, but the forces they brought are … substantial. We have to strike tomorrow, or we'll lose our chance to grab the other cities before Le Majest can disperse his troops. Defending cities is easier than taking them. We need that advantage. And the chance to turn the populations to our side before the Winged Empire's Claws march from Glorious Ingvar."

"But how can the Single Wing possibly organize that fast? We can't even get to another city in time from here."

She shook her head. "We can. There are ways. There are the gaps in the Forbidding – they fold and stretch time. We could spend days traveling down one and end up having spent only an hour of real time. There are other ways, too, but it's the paths in the gaps that we're planning to use. That's why Abghar told Chandres to think until tomorrow morning. Chandres will see sense. He won't want to lose this chance and neither do we. We go now while it's still a surprise, while we have the advantage."

I sucked in a long breath. "You say 'we' like you plan to fight."

She clenched her jaw. "We're the relentless, Aella. We will fight. Some people will stay here to guard the children, but I have no children, so I'll go. Even Alect and the boys and girls his age will go. We need everyone who can fight – even a little bit. And they need me to help anyone who is injured. I'm getting good at it, you know - healing."

She wrapped the last bandage around Osprey's wounds with hands that really were very deft, and I chewed the inside of my cheek. When I'd imagined the Single Wing fighting, I hadn't imagined boys and girls Alect's age. I'd been thinking of hardened settlers – adults, veterans.

"It's the only way," Raquella reminded me. And, of course, she was right. What other chance would we have? Especially if she was right about the troops landing in Glorious Ingvar.

I thought I heard a hitch in Osprey's breathing, but when I checked it was still long and steady. He was sleeping, at least. Safe from all of this for now.

"Then I have to be there," I said. "I can help coordinate things. My bees have power."

Someone cleared a throat and I turned to see my brothers and sisters ringed around the fire. They were quiet now that the children were tucked into their beds, but at their center was a face I wouldn't forget and two inky spirit-birds.

Victore.

I'd almost forgotten him in the middle of everything else.

"You do have to be there," he said, a strange look in his eyes. "According to prophecy, we will fail without your bees. You must be present for the attack."

CHAPTER TEN

I was surprised to see my siblings gathering around Victore and pulling up a chair for him. He sat, hunched over a small mug of tea that Raquella had hurried to put in his hands. He looked like he'd known them for months rather than just a day.

"Is this plan of the Single Wing to take everything at once yours, Victore?" I asked respectfully.

Victore looked to Adigale who smiled and patted him on a bony shoulder.

"We need the girl with the bees," he told her.

"She'll be there, grandfather," Adigale said.

Grandfather?

He looked over us all with watery eyes, not focused on anyone, and then as he stared into his tea he began to mutter. As soon as he spoke, Alect had a quill and parchment and began to write.

"Once the ships are fired you need to be off the docks. There will be chaos there as they try to put out fires. No need to stir them more. Besides, you don't want to kill citizens. Those are your allies. No, you need them on your side. Leave them to fight their battles against the flames. They can't beat them, but they must still try. That's when you secure the gatehouses and towers. Stealth is key. If you can take them without being seen, this is best. Place your teams with care. They strike the moment the flames are in the harbor. The very moment. And that is when your civilians rise up. Not to fight, no, no, to negotiate. You must corner the key people in the city – heads of merchant consortiums, sky binders, healers of repute, High'uns. Your citizens must plead with them to join us – but not right away. They make the plea when the battle is already begun, when the docks are ablaze and the towers taken, when it seems inevitable that we must win. At the same time, you have your people surrounding whoever governs and this part is messy because maybe you like the governor, but you must be decisive. If it is a council, then it draws out longer, but the same strategy applies. You give the governor a single demand and one minute to answer. Surrender or die. If he surrenders, this is good. Be very loud. Show him off as your prisoner. Make it clear the city is yours. If he does not surrender, this must also be loud. Kill him quickly and his body should be put on display so there is no doubt."

He stopped and sipped his tea and then looked up and I was stunned to see he was still glassy-eyed. "Now, where is Sorrow?"

One of his dark birds fluttered down and landed in his lap. He cooed to it, stroking the head of the bird. He offered it his teacup and the bird dipped its beak in the tea and then preened its spirit feathers.

"Is he always like this?" I whispered to Raquella as she settled next to me, but it was Alect who answered.

"Always. They have me watching him and I write down what he says. We had plans before he arrived, but they've already been modified twice. With these notes, maybe it will be a third time. He doesn't remember who he is half the time – remembers nothing of us at all – but he whispers out military strategy like breathing. Constant musings on how to take an impenetrable wall."

"Miners," Victore muttered.

"How to secure your water source."

"No rivers, they can be dammed by the enemy." He didn't even look like he was listening, but his answer was lightning fast.

"Or even how to bring the Empire to its knees."

"It's always the bees. Every time. I've gamed it out a hundred times – no a thousand – and it's always the bees in the end. That's why they wrote of them. It has to be bees."

Alect shook his head. "He's a little mad, but who could blame him? They say he's been in a tower for over a decade. His clothing was barely holding together."

He was dressed in basic clothing now – something they must have scrounged for him, though it was much too large. Anything would have been too large on a man so gaunt and hollow.

Licking my lips nervously, I stood and walked carefully over to him.

"Victore? Can you tell me how the bees are supposed to help?"

"Has to be bees."

"Yes," I said, "but how. How are the bees supposed to work?"

"Have to be there. Their buzz vibrates it all apart. Bees have a queen, see? And she runs the hive. Bites their heads off. Moves the hive. Buzzing. Always buzzing."

He wasn't making any sense now. I looked up at Adigale but she just shook her head. No one expected him to make sense out of anything other than military tactics. Eventually, he finished his tea and was brought to a pallet to sleep and I returned to Osprey's side, still worried about him and worried just as much about what Victore said. Everyone expected me to change something, but I had no idea how to do that, and tomorrow they were going to go fight. Everything would rest on me. What was I going to do?

I sat by Osprey, holding his hand, and worrying about it as the voices around me buzzed like a hive of their own.

"You need your sleep," my sister Anfrea said eventually, urging one after another off to bed. A watch had been set on rotation that included everyone but me – despite my protests that I could help. And the main room of the house was full of pallets for all of us without children of our own. The little ones were packed in tight with their parents in the quieter rooms.

My sister blew out the candles and turned down the oil lamps until there was nothing left but the lights for those on watch and the flicker of the cook fire in the grate. I curled up beside Osprey since space was tight. It wasn't the same as taking a place in his bed, it was just a place to rest on the floor where I could keep an eye on him. If it had been a real bed, my siblings would have disapproved, anyway, but I was as close to Raquella as I was to him lying here.

It worried me that he hadn't woken up yet. Worried me even more that I felt my bees burning hotter than ever. I slipped my fingers into the cuff around my wrist and felt a burst of relief at the sting of pain from their burning heat. At least I knew that his magic was still strong. That had to mean something.

I tucked a blanket gently around him, gave him a last glance over, and cuddled down into my own thin blanket.

"Guarding your prize?" Raquella whispered sleepily, but I was drifting away before she said anything more to tease me.

CHAPTER ELEVEN

I was disturbed in the night with a vision from one of my bees.

It buzzed crazily, veering one way and then the next. It took me a moment to realize it was circling Ixtap. He was with two other Hissan in a narrow stone corridor. There was barely enough room in it to turn around. He squatted there, lamp held high over a hand-drawn map in a hand that looked vaguely familiar. It showed a large building the size of a palace and in tiny notes and a careful hand it seemed to indicate hidden ways to move through the place. Ixtap traced one with his finger as his followers looked over his shoulder.

I waited for the vision to leave me, but this time, it didn't. My bee followed as they crept through the narrow corridor to where a door was bolted from the inside. Ixtap didn't open the bolt, instead, he reached a dagger tip through a tiny peephole and pushed cloth aside to peer in the room beyond. And then a green glow lit the corridor as he manifested his adder.

I woke with a gasp.

Beside me, Osprey stirred gently and gasped. I put my hand on his chest and felt my bee. The burning was fading and the bee was hard at work, repairing.

Gently, I eased back his blindfold and his eyes flickered open.

"We're in a house in a Single Wing outpost," I whispered to

him, as quietly as I could. "With my family. You're safe."

Beside me, Raquella stirred. Even my whisper was too loud. He turned on his side to face me and I lay down again, this time, on my side so that our noses were only inches apart. My heart was too loud. I felt like the whole room could hear it. Just being so close to him made the feather in my chest ache.

"My bees have stopped burning. I can feel them repairing what's inside. I think … I think you're free."

"House Apidae," he said, like my name was honey. But I didn't hear the rest. I was rocked with another vision. I reached out to him without meaning to, grabbing his arm with my hand as the vision shook me.

Ixtap's snake was through the little peek hole, slithering into a huge room, decadent with silk screens. An entire wall was carved in white feathers with water flowing over them into a pool where live swans swam lazily in the moonlight.

The snake slithered past them, growing in size as it filled the room, loop on loop. It ignored the reading stand and the table decked in fresh blooms and fruit. It slid past the wide balcony carved with herons in white marble. It slid up to a dais where a wide bed was laid with silken sheets and someone lay tangled in the sheets – heavy and thick of limb, his back to us, his arms tangled through the sheets. Beyond him on a small settee stitched in bird wing brocade, discarded clothing lay crumpled partially covering the white-gold gleam of the Wing Crown.

Ixtap's spirit snake undulated back and forth before the sleeping man as I blinked against nausea from my bee swinging frantically back and forth like a pendulum. I fought to keep my eyes focused, fought to see through them – and then immediately regretted it. The snake's mouth opened impossibly large at the same moment that the sleeper awoke, opened his eyes – his brilliant blue eyes, blue even in the moonlight – and screamed.

The sound didn't even sound human. It sounded like something from deep within the belly of an animal and it went on and on as the spirit snake struck, swallowing the man in a series of spasmodic gulps. Someone was yelling in the background. Someone was pounding on the door. The scream was muffled now as the spirit snake closed its mouth and faded, his victim fading with him so that when the Swan Claws burst into the room, weapons held high, there was nothing left for them to see.

I didn't realize that there were tears of horror running down my face until Osprey moved to wipe them away with his bound hands.

"House Apidae?" he whispered.

I blinked away my tears. Should I tell him? Probably not right now. He had enough on his mind – and I didn't know for sure. I mean, I'd never seen the Emperor before. Maybe there were other people out there with Winged crowns and silken bed chambers. Maybe that was the lover of the Emperor and not the Emperor himself – or the maker of crowns. Or a hundred other people. But in my heart, I knew that was not true.

"Osprey," I whispered, and I felt my bee resonate with my whisper. It felt – free. Clear. It was working hard, and I felt it drawing from my strength and … his? But it was working, repairing, helping. I sighed with relief. "You're free … aren't you?"

And that meant that even if that was the emperor who had died – if my vision was real – then he wouldn't die, too.

His smile was like a golden dawn. He lifted his head and then immediately slumped again. "Free and weak as a newborn chick.

But still free. I can feel where the binding was – like an empty spot. Like something that's gone missing."

I bit my lip. Had my bees done more than they should have? "Do you feel a loss?"

He was quick to shake his head and then wince. "I don't, but I can't help but ache at the thought that the innocents I've been protecting are now unprotected. While my heart was held ransom, they had some protection. No one would kill them without a cause because they were needed. But now … what will happen to them now? I have to go to them, House Apidae. I have to ensure their safety."

"You will," I whispered. "But not tonight. Rest for tonight. You need to heal."

"I can hardly lift my head," he said, laughing grimly and quietly. "I'm not even sure I can do that much."

Gently, I reached for his hands, working the knots loose on his bonds and freeing them. They found my waist almost immediately, drawing me to him in a way that made my heart quicken within me.

"You freed me, Aella of House Apidae," he whispered reverently. "I owe my freedom to you. It feels … I can't describe the feeling of having my heart to myself. Although it's not really my own any longer. It belongs entirely to you. You've redeemed what is yours. You've bought my will from my captor and my body from the rule of Le Majest. They are yours forever."

I watched his lips as he spoke, hardly believing that this could be true. After so many times that he had to follow that up with hurt, this time, he simply held me like a piece of pottery too fragile to trust to anyone else. One thumb stroked my waist and the warmth of his hands bled through my clothing and filled me with little shivers that had nothing to do with the temperature of the air.

He tried to lean forward and then snorted a laugh at himself when he didn't have the strength for even that.

"I should give you the brew the healer sent," I whispered.

"Please, not yet," he pled through those gorgeous curved lips. "Those things always make you sleep, and I want to drink you in, if only for a few more moments. In my life, very few things have truly been mine to hold and keep, and what few things I have had, have all been ripped from my grasp. But this moment is mine. It's a treasure beyond what I could reasonably have hoped for. Or unreasonably."

My breath caught and I bit my lip again, this time feeling suddenly self-conscious. That he was choosing to make this his moment – to give himself fully to me – it felt like too much, like something I wasn't worthy to receive, and yet I wanted it so desperately, I couldn't turn him down. Not for a second.

I leaned in gently and kissed him – softly, carefully, savoring the sweetness of his lips and the way they melded to mine like we were two halves meant to fit together. Sweet agony seared me as the feather in my chest rebelled, seizing my heart and making it beat arrhythmically so that my breathing grew difficult and pain seared through my breast. And yet, I wasn't willing to stop. Not even to spare myself the pain.

I drew back long enough for a breath and Osprey was smiling – a rare thing for him. The sight of it nearly broke my heart.

"House Apidae," he whispered.

"Yes?"

"I think I'll take that nickname now."

I paused a moment, thinking. “I’ll call you Hunter because that was what you were – the hunter who started to chase my spirit but eventually won my heart.”

“I didn’t plan that,” he protested.

“Complain in the morning. Right now, you take your medicine.”

It was harder than I could have imagined to will myself to slip from his grasp but I was careful not to wake anyone as I found the herbs the healer had given me and mixed them with water. I helped him lift his head to drink.

“House Apidae,” he whispered to me when he was finished.

“Hunter?” I teased.

His dimple showed at that. “Lie here with me as I fall asleep?”

“Of course,” I said, slipping down beside him and twining my fingers through his. “You should know,” I said awkwardly, “that while my loyalties and my heart have been spoken for against my will, they are yours. Yours entirely.”

He sighed contentedly and winked at me.

I leaned in to kiss him and found he was kissing me with more energy than I thought he had. I fought to stay silent as I kissed him, so I wouldn’t wake anyone else in the crowded room. But when I kissed him back, I poured my whole heart into those silent kisses as if there would never be another chance for more. And there might not be. Not when tomorrow morning meant revolution. And I was needed at that revolution. I should probably have told him that, but I was far too engrossed in what we were doing, on the scent and taste of him, on this intense intimacy I hadn’t dared hope for. By the time I thought I might have the willpower to stop, his kisses were slowing sleepily, and then our lips parted and he snuggled into his blankets, his lips still moving slightly as if he thought he was kissing me as he drifted into a drugged sleep.

I sighed with regret. I had the feeling that no matter how many kisses I had from him, they would never be enough.

Awet popped his head in the door just as I was starting to drift off. There were sounds from outside. I was instantly awake and sitting up, sending a quick glance to Osprey and was relieved when I saw his relaxed face and deep breathing.

"Chandres is here. Get Abghar," Awet whispered to me before leaving again and closing the door.

I picked my way through the sleeping bodies to the room on the main floor where Abghar and his wife and children were sleeping. It had been a large pantry before, and it was packed tight with bodies. It took only the faintest whisper and my oldest brother was up. I looked away as he kissed each of his little ones and his wife and then I followed him through the dark house through the back door and into the sharp cold of the night.

CHAPTER TWELVE

I closed the door quietly behind me when I saw who was there, wishing I'd brought my swords instead of leaving them beside Osprey. Chandres was front and center with Wing Essena looking smug beside him and around them were the other faces I'd seen at the table last night. The heads of the Houses represented here – grim-faced men and women, some looking slightly ashamed of themselves, others calculating and distant.

It took me a moment to realize that Abghar had snatched up a mug of cold tea left out last night and a half-eaten roll on his way out the door. He leaned against the house and took a bite of the roll, the picture of sanguine calm, both hands so full he couldn't draw a weapon in time if he were attacked.

"Light a lamp sister," he nodded to a lantern placed on the front step and then to one lit above the door. "Our guests may prefer to move in the dark, but I like shedding light on the situation."

I moved to obey, puzzled at first, but when I saw the uncertainty in the faces of those who had come to confront us, it made sense. This show of calm took them by surprise. It was hard to rail on someone who was this confident and this friendly. Who didn't have a weapon, just a half-eaten roll and a mug of cold tea. I lit the lamp with care and held it up as they spoke.

"You left the decision to us, House Shrike. You closed ranks and left with distrust in your hearts."

Abghar took a long sip of the cold tea, appearing to enjoy it. "We don't turn on our own, Chandres. You should know that. We still plan to fight just as we all planned."

"With her beside you? The wife of Le Majest?" Chandres's words got louder as he spoke.

"If you don't mind, my children are sleeping in that house and I'd prefer to keep them asleep," Abghar said, taking another sip of tea for all the world as if he was unaffected. Beside us, Awet was practically vibrating he was so tense. I tried to copy Abghar's feigned ease, holding the lamp in a steady hand.

"If that is your stance, House Shrike, you must know what our response will be," he hissed.

"Gratitude?" Abghar suggested. "Between us, House Shrike is the key to three of the battles the Single Wing plans to launch and we are also offering eight strong fighters including a Wing. Have you even consulted the leaders in the other encampments?"

He didn't look at me as he spoke, but all of them didn't take their eyes off me. Essena's eyes were dark with hate but the others were watching me with consideration.

"We can't have a traitor in our ranks," Chandres said firmly.

"Then what do you suggest?" Abghar bit the roll to punctuate his sentence.

Chandres looked to Essena and my heart sank. This was her plan. And that couldn't be a good thing.

"None of us wants bad blood, House Shrike," he said with a slight smile as if he couldn't quite disguise how clever he thought he was. "Since you won't send your sister out of camp and since you insist on joining the battle to come, we won't stop you. But we have revised our plans to keep House Shrike from turning on us. We expect that you will still send Oska and Royn to the cities they are slated to take. They have the contacts there that we need. But now we want to see the rest of your family divided among the battles. If one of you turns on any part of this plan, all of you will suffer."

"We have no argument with that," Abghar said mildly. He threw the last bite of his roll to the ground and seemed surprised when it bounced and landed on Essena's toe. Her eyes narrowed and it was all I could do not to laugh. Abghar had perfect aim. There was no way that was an accident.

Chandres nodded happily but the shifting of the people behind him told me he wasn't finished. One of the women – a woman with grosbeaks decorating her cape and a long scar on her brow that went into her hairline – had the grace to look embarrassed as he spoke again.

"And we've put Glorious Ingvar back on the table. We want you to lead that foray. With your sister – the bride of Le Majest – and Wing Essena as your crew."

Abghar stilled so suddenly that I was worried he was in pain. His words came out tight and careful.

"We took Glorious Ingvar off the table when word reached us of the early revolt there. The place is under martial law. All our people there have been executed."

"All cities are under martial law now that Le Majest has sent out his birds. And not everyone was executed. We've heard from two of our contacts. They still live."

"A fleet of ships have just docked there unloading hundreds of Claw reinforcements and all our networks and supply routes are compromised," Abghar reminded him.

"All the more reason to secure the city, don't you think?" Chandres said coldly, and now Essena really was smiling. Her owl appeared on her shoulder and it seemed to be laughing at us.

"I do not think," Abghar said distinctly. "It's a fools' errand. Why would you risk Wing Essena if you are certain she is not a traitor?"

"Wing Essena can take care of herself."

As if on cue, Essena extended her arm and her owl appeared, blinking at us before it lifted from her arm and began to circle over our heads. I resisted the urge to look up. That's what she wanted – to unsettle us. To make us doubt.

A torch flared from behind Chandres. And then two more.

"What will it be, House Shrike? A fools' errand or fire to your house? Did you say your children were sleeping in there?"

I gasped, my knees suddenly jelly. I'd expected them to ask me to do something hard. I hadn't expected this.

"You're supposed to be the good ones," I choked out.

Abghar's eyes flicked to mine, compassion filling them. He felt sorry for me. Why? It took a moment for the answer to come to me and then my cheeks flared hot. He felt sad that I was such a fool that I still believed there were good ones at all. I swallowed down a feeling of shame mixed with misery.

"Of course, I'll go," I said immediately. All of this had been to protect my family and Osprey – not put all of them in mortal danger. "But why would you ask Abghar to go on a suicide mission?"

Abghar cleared his throat loudly. "My little sister does not speak for House Shrike."

My mouth fell open and beside me, Awet drew his sword with a rasping sound. He'd been silent this whole time, steady, eyes watching the shadows. My heart hurt just looking at him. He shouldn't have to be disillusioned any more than I should have to be.

"Then do speak, Head of House," Essena said, mockery in her tone.

In answer, Abghar threw the rest of his cold tea on the ground, raising his eyebrows when it splashed on Essena's toes. Her face stiffened and Abghar turned to me.

"You are certain, sister?"

I nodded, not trusting my voice. I would do what I had to. I would be relentless, and I would save my family.

He nodded sharply, pride shining in his eyes. He looked so much like the old man like that. It hurt my heart.

"Then I will go with you and we will pay this steep price for the doubts of these lily-livered dogs we've been calling friends." He turned to them. "We will go, but I will have you bound to this vow. You will not hurt my family – not one member – nor cause them to be hurt. This threat you've made today breaks all our previous bonds and ties. We will fight this one battle because we believe in it, but you will not hold us beyond that or harm a hair of our heads – on your blood."

"There's no sky binder here to hold us to that vow," Chandres said silkily.

Abghar smirked. "Perhaps not, but that's a raven's beak around your neck, is it not, Chandres? And I'm no fool. I've seen that charm before, and I know its purpose. If we all put our blood on it with our oath it will bind us. And I will have your vow before we part. I will enact the rebellion in Glorious Ingvar and you will not touch a hair of my House's heads. And that includes the heads of Zayana, Wing Ivo, Wing Osprey, and General Victore who are under my roof and under the protection of my house."

Chandres face was a thunderbolt now and Essena had gone very white. Would they back out? It was a clever maneuver by Abghar.

However Chandres had gathered the others with him, they could hardly be expected to back him if he pressed Abghar after Abghar had given him everything he asked for. The woman in the grosbeak cloak reached forward and snatched the beak charm from around Chandres' throat, stepping to a spot equidistant between their group and ours. She cut her hand quickly with her knife, pressing it to the beak.

"On my honor and blood, House Grosbeak will not harm a hair of the heads of House Shrike, if House Shrike fulfills their bargain made tonight."

Abghar didn't hesitate. He threw down his tin mug and strode forward, slicing his own palm with his belt knife before grasping her palm in his, the beak between them.

"On my honor and blood, House Shrike will fulfill our commitment to send our family to fight the Winged Empire as we have promised, if these houses vow not to lay a hand on my family or those under my protection."

The others behind Chandres joined them one by one. House Chickadee, House Plover, House Nuthatch, House Quail, House Thrush and on and on until eventually a grim Chandres and a jaw-clenching Essena joined them and then it was done.

"You leave at first light," Chandres said, snatching back his pendant.

"As do we all," Abghar agreed.

My mouth was dry as they left us. Dry because I was worried for our family even with this bargain meant to protect them. Dry because all was not as I had hoped. Dry because Abghar had taken this risk for me and I must take it, too. The last place I ever wanted to return to was Glorious Ingvar and the husband who waited for me there.

When at last they were out of earshot, Abghar seemed to sag with relief, but he turned to us both with a grim smile and planted a hand on each of our shoulders.

"I'm proud of you both," he said in his deep voice so like my father's, "and so would our parents be had they lived to see what fine young people you are. What are we?"

"Relentless," Awet whispered, though his voice quavered. He knew as well as I did what kind of risk we would be taking tomorrow. Even more so now. Our family would fight in every battle. Which meant more chances that one of us would not return. And we would have to leave our most vulnerable members behind and hope beyond hope that the blood oath held.

"Relentless," I said, trying to keep the waver out of my voice.

But I hadn't succeeded. Abghar grabbed us each with one of his huge arms, pulling us in for a tight, furious hug. And even he was trembling a little when he let us go.

"Try to get some sleep," he advised. "Dawn will be difficult."

CHAPTER THIRTEEN

Dawn was difficult as Abghar had predicted. I'd managed to catch an hour of sleep cuddled next to Osprey but as the first rays of gold appeared over the horizon, I rose with the others, drinking tea hastily, checking weapons, packing supplies. I left Osprey's swords with him and as the others ate a quick breakfast, I sat cross-legged beside my sleeping hunter and opened my palms, whispering to my bees. Their buzz filled me, and I leaned into it.

"Come to me, my swarm," I whispered. "I need you now. You're a family just as my House is a family. But now we must go our separate ways and I need you to go with them. You are my heart and my hopes. Fly with my family. Warn them of danger. Set yourselves as watch holders and flare brightly in the presence of evil so they can be warned. And stay connected to your swarm. Keep me connected to my family so I can know if they succeed or fall, know their hearts and struggles. Be my eyes. Be my ears. Be my voice of encouragement."

I blew gently on the golden swarm and they scattered through the room, landing on shoulders, or spinning haloed loops around the heads of my family.

Anfrea looked up with a faintly amused look in her eye and Retger swatted irritably at his, but the bees weren't going anywhere. I kissed Osprey's cheek, trying hard not to think of it as goodbye. He was deep in drugged sleep. If all went well, he wouldn't wake until I returned. Then I rose and joined the huddled ring in the kitchen. Tension painted every face and while Retger and Oska were putting on brave faces, Helissa was crying a little, clutching her husband like she feared he might never return.

"I've set my bees to watch you for me," I said.

"Not necessary," Retger grumbled.

"They'll flare very bright if they sense danger."

He snorted at that but seemed mollified. Raquella tilted her head and reached for the bee curiously, seeming delighted when it landed on her hand and walked up her arm.

"Can I pray?" I asked and wordlessly we huddled around as I reached out like I had before in the undertrails and then in the tower, stretching my heart up to feel that presence up and beyond the sky and stars. "Flight of wind protect us, mercy of the skies fly over us, give us peace and protection, let us soar from this terror on the wings of eagles. Guide us in the right paths. Give us courage to face today."

My voice faltered, but Adigale picked up the prayer in her strong voice. "In the ever-changing nature of life, in the storms and stillness, shine your light on us."

And then the tear-thick voice of Helissa joined her, "Grant us peace in this time of trouble."

And when she was finished there was a flurry of hugs and whispered goodbyes and I could hardly manage to keep the tears from falling. It felt like it was tearing me in two to leave them when I'd only just been returned to them.

"We'll look after your injured friend," Helissa assured me as she hugged me goodbye. "Come back quickly and maybe he won't even wake until you return."

Raquella snorted. "Friend. Is that what we're calling it?"

Helissa gave her a censorious look. "And you be careful, Raquella. It would be just like you to tie up your own poor captive and drag him back here."

And then we were being handed small parcels of food and waterskins and we were checking our weapons quietly.

"We're in a tough position," Abghar announced quietly. "But today will be a decisive blow one way or another. Those who remain here are essential. You need to keep the children safe and watch over our injured allies – Wing Ivo and Wing Osprey. You also need to protect General Victore. Let's hope he regains his mind."

Adigale made a murmur in the back of her throat that suggested it was unlikely.

"We've tried to leave as many behind as we can," Abghar continued. "And they've split us up which leaves us all nervous, but here are my last words to you. Those of you who are staying behind, Anfrea has taken charge of the defenses here and she will give the final call if you must leave this place or withdraw to another. We will all return here or send word here as soon as we are able, to set our family's minds at rest. Whichever battle each of us finds ourselves fighting in, the rest of our hearts are with you. If you are taken, we will come after you. If you fall …" he paused. "Don't fall. And now, we depart."

He kissed his wife and we followed him grimly out into the half-light of dawn. Little tendrils of mist rose from the ground as the warmth of dawn began to spread over the cold earth.

We clasped hands in goodbye as Oska peeled off to the side

with Raquella to join a group assembling where the archery butts had been last night.

“Don’t think I didn’t hear you two last night,” she whispered in my ear, making an over-enthusiastic kissy sound with a wink as she left.

Royn was next to leave us with Alect. I gave my younger brother a tight hug.

“Be safe,” I murmured, and he winked, too, as he trotted off behind Royn’s wide figure, striding toward where a group of about thirty was already assembled near the fletcher’s workshop.

And then it was our turn. I hugged everyone and caught Zayana’s eye from where she stood in Retger’s shadow. She hardly seemed to leave his side.

“I’ve barely had a chance to talk to you,” I told her. “Will you be okay?”

She sniffed like I was being ridiculous. “I’ll be safer than you. I have Retger and we’ve been chosen for one of the easier tasks. You, on the other hand, are as suicidal as you’ve always been.”

“I prefer the word ‘brave,’” I said with a smile and then Abghar was motioning me to hurry and I gave her a hug and hurried to catch up with him. His face was grim as we left the others.

“I’m sorry that you’ve been put in this difficult spot because of me,” I whispered as we strode over a little bridge that spanned the creek. I could see Essena waiting for us near the gap where I’d entered with Osprey. Her owl was on her shoulder, glowing a milky white.

“I make my own choices, Shrikeling,” he said, sparing me a half-smile. “Don’t feel guilt for what I decide to do.”

"Just … you have to make it back here to your family," I whispered, nervous suddenly. "Whatever happens to me, you need to promise you'll get out safely."

"Like I said, I make my own choices."

And that was all he was willing to say. We walked the rest of the way to Essena in silence and with every step, I grew more and more nervous. What would be there on the other side of the gap? Would Essena betray us immediately, or wait until it was too late to escape? Acid filled my mouth, and I was glad I hadn't eaten breakfast as my stomach twisted within me.

Relentless, Aella, be relentless.

I'd just had a sweet reminder of all the reasons I was fighting. I didn't dare lose my nerve now.

Essena's owl flew over us as we approached her – far too close for comfort. Its talons almost scraped my shoulders as it hovered there, and her smile was placid when we joined her – though it never reached her eyes.

"We should begin immediately. There are horses waiting for us on the other side of the gap," she said smoothly.

"I thought you knew nothing about the Forbidding," I said. I was trying to reconcile this Essena with the cool, informational Essena I'd known before the Forbidding caught our caravan near Vlaren, but it was hard to do. What had happened to her that day?

"You can learn so much in a single encounter with something, don't you think?" Still, her smile didn't touch her eyes.

When I'd entered the undertrails they had kneaded and folded me into more somehow. And again, in the tower, more of who I was had been teased to the surface. Had the same thing happened to Essena? Had she become more of herself and had it made her into this steely-eyed woman?

"How will the others get to where they are going?" I asked Abghar. "And how can we all get there in time?"

He looked at the Forbidding as we stepped toward the gap and his face held all the worry and wonder that I knew was on my own.

"All these years, and we never realized how powerful the magic of this place is. This thing we call the gap bends and folds time and space. It will take us to where we're going, we just need to step in the right spot and this path marks that spot. There are other trails leading from the encampment that go to other gaps. Each party will take the right one. I have a map in my bag, but we don't need it. It's a simple thing to walk to the gap."

"When Marcel led us in, we were a full day or more journey to Glorious Ingvar," I said, eyeing the gap suspiciously.

"Yes," he agreed. "When we enter the gap, we'll take a turn, and it will bring us closer to the city."

"I don't remember any turns on the way here," I said suspiciously.

"The things you don't know and don't remember could fill a very long book," Essena said sharply. "You still have those bees buzzing around you willy nilly, despite my attempts to teach you control. They're a clear sign to anyone watching that you still have a lot to learn – about magic and about the dark magic known as the Forbidding."

"And are you going to teach me?" I asked wryly. "I would think that since you wanted me dead this morning, you wouldn't waste your time."

"I do not want you dead. Nor do I want you to remain ignorant," she said in a voice so cold it could have been used to chill drinks in summer. But I didn't believe her. She wanted something more from me than just stirring up the camp. She'd planned all this to get us away from everyone else. But if I was careful, perhaps I could keep her from getting what she wanted.

We set out on the path and immediately my stomach lurched as the path banked sharply to the side and then seemed to spiral over itself. I kept my eyes focused straight ahead and tried not to be ill as we followed in single-file down the path. What worried me even more than the nausea-inducing path was that the pain in my feather eased slightly as if my body were glad to be headed back toward Juste Montpetit.

I was greeted – as if the vision was summoned by that thought – with an immediate view from Juste's honeycomb. He was walking down a line of Claws standing in military parade. They looked very crisp in their blue jackets with the white swans embroidered heavily across shoulders and chests. I barely had time to register more than the sheer numbers of them when I swayed back into my body again.

Abghar had me held by the elbow. "Are you hurt, Aella?"

"No," I said with a gasp. "But if I stumble like that again, please keep my feet on the path. It happens from time to time."

"If she's going to faint, perhaps we should leave her here and carry on without her," Essena said with mock sympathy in her voice.

"Leave her on the path in the gap?" Abghar's tone made it clear that he'd never do that.

"It was only a kind suggestion," Essena said and the little flicker of movement around her mouth told me she was testing him.

That wasn't what had me worried. The sheer number of Claws he had assembled in Glorious Ingvar was what made me feel ill. How were we supposed to get around them and also avoid the curfew restrictions? There was no point in mentioning it. Aghar already knew we'd been sent on a quest that was more intended to kill us than to achieve anything, and Essena would gladly turn me over to the Claws in a heartbeat. Perhaps, we'd be lucky, and we could find a way to slip from her grasp on our way into the city.

After what felt like an hour, we reached a sprawling oak tree that was tangled by the Forbidding – its branches reaching out like waving tentacles and a huge hole in its trunk that seemed to almost dance and waver if you looked at it for too long. I noted the tree – and noted it again when we passed the exact same tree a second time. Abghar paused and turned us all around going back the same way we'd come.

"Are we lost?" I asked.

"That was the turn," he said as if it was perfectly understandable to walk a distance and then turn and go back the same way. He looked at me sympathetically. "None of it makes any sense. But it works. You'll have to trust me."

I did trust him. And it wouldn't have mattered if I didn't. The Forbidding was whispering in the back of my head.

FOLD. BEND. FIND THE WAY. YOU ARE UNDER JUDGMENT.

I tried to ignore it, but it only grew louder as if the mind of the Forbidding was trying to reach me the way the tentacles had reached for me before.

A PIECE OF US IN EVERY HEART.

Another vision gripped me as I was still struggling to buck the voice of the Forbidding. I was just lucid enough to keep stumbling along with Abghar supporting me as my bee transmitted back to me what it was seeing.

Ixtap and his men were in that stone corridor again – waiting. One leaned against the stone wall, face upturned, chanting something in near silence. Another carefully cleaned his teeth with a carved bone pick. Ixtap had his eye to a tiny peephole. He was utterly silent. Watching. Waiting.

I almost jumped when he suddenly sprang into action. He jammed his hand against a protruding rock in the wall and that portion of it swung outward.

Without having to be ordered, his men fell in behind him and his snake poured from his hand, enlarging into a massive creature as it shot out from him into the decadent room beyond. He was almost as quick as it was, darting in behind on quick feet, head held high, arms raised up as if conducting a religious ceremony.

This was not the bedroom of the emperor anymore, but even having never been there, I knew exactly what it was. I knew by the high stained glass ceiling – so high that you could have fit five of my homestead between the pale marble floor and the jewel-toned ceiling designed from diamond slices of glass the size of my palm. Yellows and blues dominated the design but there were cherry reds and bright dawn pinks in there, as one bird designed of diamond glass panes flowed into another swooping bird design which fit into another yet. Even in the Far Stones, I'd heard rumors of Levard Le Pateur the great artist who had spent fifteen years on the throne room ceiling, designing the perfect interlace of bird and bird that left not a single space for a patch of sky, so skillful was his design. He'd gone mad in the last year of the work and his journeyman helper had finished the final leading.

Hearing the story and seeing it in person were two entirely different things. I barely held in my gasp at how the ceiling flowed down into the reaching feathers and wings of the marble support pillars. They were slender and ethereal, the buttressing disguised by carved marble wings so that the whole of the support system looked as if it might take flight in a moment. Even those who had placed the marble of the floor had turned their mind to birds. There was not an avian in all the world who was not represented somewhere in the branching designs of the floor – and there at the head of the room with latticed arches behind it leading to the aviary and the magnificent rare birds imported from every nation conquered by the Winged Empire – there stood the Winged Throne. White with delicate gilding and just the slightest blush in the seat like the heart of a lily, the throne rose high over the gathered people. Standing just under it, a Heron – one of the Winged Empire's crown advisors and a pair of Vultures stood grimly detailing the disappearance of the emperor to his assembled court. Their spirit birds stood watch over them – but despite their large spectral forms and the sheer numbers of High'uns gathered – they seemed a small group in the sheer size of the throne room.

None of them saw Ixtap's snake approaching. They were too filled with their own anxieties and fears. But when his footsteps rang across the stone, then they looked up and horror filled their eyes. I couldn't look away. It was like being in a nightmare – knowing disaster was about to strike – and yet unable to do anything to turn the tide.

One of the spirit birds – a pelican – dove for the snake at the same time that the Skybinder opened her mouth.

"This court is closed to visitors."

The snake struck, snatching the pelican from the air and sucking it down with a single gulp.

The Skybinder flinched, her face going suddenly white, and her hands trembling so much that the Vultures beside her had to step past her, hands raised in defense. Around the perimeter of the room, Claws sprang into action rushing forward as the spirit-vultures in their inky black-on-black glowing darkness burst from the hands of their manifestors and shot toward Ixtap.

He raised a hand in a sign that could have meant peace or simply a refusal.

“Enough of these displays.” His voice was quiet, but it seemed to fill the room even as one of the other snakes of the Hissan snatched a running Claw up and swallowed him in a single gulp. There was no bulge in the snake where he could be – no sign that the spirit snake had ever swallowed a Claw at all. “I come here as the envoy of Juste Montpetit, Le Majest, son of the Emperor, Lord of the Winged Empire, Chosen of the Hissan. Would you slay the envoy of your lord?”

The Claws’ progress forward slowed as they looked to the vultures whose birds swept up, disentangling from the snakes to circle above instead.

An Owl stepped from the crowd of advisors, his chin wavering as he spoke for them, eyes darting to the Vultures and the Skybinder and then back to Ixtap.

“We are prostrate before Le Majest, the crown jewel of the empire, and today of all days we long for his presence among us, for his father has been taken and we know not where he has gone.”

Ixtap smiled coldly. “He has gone to his ancestors, old man. As did his father before him.”

The Owl swallowed visibly, his eyes darting around the room as if he was looking for someone else to help him decide what to do. After a moment, he shook his head very quickly and looked to Ixtap.

"We need some proof that you are his envoy. For though you are doubtless honorable in your intentions." Some of the crowd shuffled uncomfortably at that. "We cannot give the heart of our Empire to any but Le Majest."

"I am told that your Skybinders can feel the essence of a person through things that were once theirs – part of them, if you will," he said, reaching into his vest and pulling out something dark and silky. He held it up – a lock of curling black hair.

The Owl glanced back at the Skybinder who was on her knees, her face in her hands. "I'm afraid our lady Pelican will no longer be able to perform such actions. A shame about her bird, wouldn't you say?"

Ixtap's face was like rock.

The Owl shook his head, still not sure what to do with a man who refused to have any of the correct reactions. "I shall test your hair myself."

He held out a hand and a small owl appeared in it. He whispered to the owl and it leapt from his grasp, swooping in a wide arc and snatching the lock of hair from Ixtap's hand. He circled back to the Owl and perched there as the old man closed his eyes.

After a long moment, they opened.

"It is the hair of Juste Montpetit, taken from his living self."

The court sighed and Ixtap took a single step forward. "Then, perhaps we can dispense with the violence?"

The Owl tilted his head and waved a hand. The Claws drew back, and the Vultures' spirit birds landed on their shoulders. One of them snapped his fingers and a servant hurried to usher the Pelican away as she sobbed. Her hands were completely empty, her bird gone forever.

"On behalf of Le Majest, Juste Montpetit, I claim the throne of the Winged Empire," Ixtap said. His spirit snake returned to him, rearing up behind him so that it was halfway to the vaulted ceiling. Around him, the court gasped, but whether from what he was doing or what he was saying, or simply out of abject terror, I couldn't tell.

I broke from the vision, my mouth dry, my whole body shaking. Had I really just seen that? Ixtap had claimed the throne for Juste after murdering his father. I guess now I knew why they spent so much time talking back in the jungle together. After all, they'd had a neat little coup to arrange together.

I gasped, clutching the arm of the person holding me. Something wasn't right. It wasn't Abghar holding me up, but a grim-faced Wing Essena.

I recoiled like I'd been slapped.

CHAPTER FOURTEEN

She rolled her eyes. "Don't be so dramatic. It's not like I'm going to kill you."

"Where's Abghar?" I asked, finding my water skin with shaking hands and taking a quick drink.

"Getting the cart," she said. "We've come through the gap."

FOLDED. BENDED. KNEADED. CHANGED.

I shook my head to dislodge the whispers of the Forbidding and I looked around, taking in long breaths to calm myself. We were standing behind a low barn in the pre-dawn of morning. I could have sworn it had taken hours for us to get here, but I would have been wrong. Or at least, we'd traveled for hours, but in the outside world, the sun was just creeping over the horizon.

In the distance, the walls of Glorious Ingvar rose. They were close. If Abghar really had a cart, it would barely take us till mid-morning to ride to the city.

"You should be working more on speaking to your manifestation," Essena said with a sniff. "You might still be able to change the way it presents itself."

"What do you care?" I asked. "You're here as a spy for Le Majest. You aren't even with your apprentices. Didn't you have some waiting for you in Astar Harbor?"

"I have work to do here," she hissed. I knew what that work was. She was a spy for the crown prince. Why else would she be here ingratiating herself with the rebels while also driving them apart? I didn't trust her and just because I couldn't figure out her purpose didn't mean she didn't have one. "And I didn't break your precious older brother's rules, so your family doesn't have blood feud with me."

She was right. She'd left the gap before dawn was finished breaking. She'd met Abghar's demands. I found it interesting that she mentioned that. Perhaps she knew I was more powerful than she was pretending I was. Perhaps she didn't want me to be more of an enemy than I already was.

It turned out that Abghar's plan to get us into the city involved hiding in a hatch under a higgler's cart – both of us but not Essena.

"They won't recognize you," he said by way of explanation to her. "Especially if you can keep your bird hidden. They're looking for Aella and maybe for someone who looks like me but not for you."

The fit in the hatch was uncomfortable and with us both squished together in the false bottom, it felt impossible to breathe. But I felt better about being in this little place with Abghar than I would have up in the cart with Essena.

The eggs were placed carefully above us and after that, there was no getting out until we made it to our destination. Just the thought of that made me worried. And just getting worried made me need to get out and take a breath.

I held myself together by breathing deeply.

"What were those spells you were having on the gap trail?" Abghar whispered to me when the cart was rolling down the road easily and the bumps weren't so bad that they rattled our bones.

It was dark in the little compartment and every muscle in my body hurt from the way we bounced on the hard wood.

"My bees show me visions," I whispered. "I saw what was happening in the capital of the Winged Empire."

"Did you see the emperor?" he asked.

"The emperor is dead," I hissed, not able to hold back my fear.

"And why is that a bad thing?" he whispered back.

"Because his son is my husband." Just admitting that felt like drinking something bitter. I hated the thought of being tied to Juste in any way and marriage was the most personal way possible. I should have told Osprey all of this before I left. I should have woken him up and made him listen.

"We can't talk about that right now," he whispered. "There are ears that hear everything."

Abghar was silent as the cart jostled us and I slipped back into the stream of visions.

Retger and Zayana slipping out of the gap and sneaking into the woods. Anfrea singing to the children, looking worriedly out the window and trying to disguise her worry for the little eyes looking at her. Osprey, still fast asleep but now with Victore sitting beside him, feeding his ravens. Raquella – looking fierce – her face framed by the city gate she was walking through.

As grateful as I was to see them safe, as the hours passed, I only worried more. I saw them in little glimpses. A look in Raquella's eye as she slipped into an alley, the confidence of Oska striding out onto the docks dressed as a sailor. Young Alect whistling as he unloaded a cart.

And still, Osprey slept.

I wondered if I should have told him that his father had been killed. And I worried that he wasn't sleeping at all. What if he had died from my bees and their work and I just couldn't tell because the snapshots were so quick?

I was getting more anxious by the second, and Essena's muttering from above us on the seat of the cart was not helping.

"Stay strong, my owl, watch for anyone with a heart who does not love the right way – the pure way – the way of glory – and eviscerate that person. We shall expose and reduce them to ash. We shall winnow and burn."

Why did the Single Wing think she was on their side? Hadn't they heard whispers like that before? Sure, she was strengthening her bird – but for what? I didn't believe for a second that she was doing any of it to help them. I'd never seen someone so obsessed with the Empire – unless it was Xectare – and I was certain she'd only come to undermine Abghar and me – or possibly kill us while we were trying to start the overthrow in this city.

"What are the three of us supposed to do?" I whispered to Abghar. "In the other cities, they have a plan for taking the towers and the wall but there are only three of us on this mission."

"We're supposed to be a distraction," Abghar whispered, bringing his lips close to my ear so that the sound wouldn't make it up into the cart. "In the original plan, this attack was meant to keep Le Majest's forces here instead of running off other places to reinforce them. When we get close to the city, I'll drop this hatch and the two of us will fall out the bottom and slip into the crowds before Essena notices."

"Really?" I whispered back. Relief filled me at the thought of being rid of her.

"I believe you, Aella. I know she is a threat. We've been sent here to die, not to achieve anything. No one expects us to make it back. They must have sent her, too, to get rid of all the discordant voices in one blow. But you and I will prove them all wrong. Relentless."

"Relentless," I agreed.

After that, it seemed like no time before we heard guards talking to the crowd and investigating the egg cart. I held my breath, watching Abghar's worried expression through the dim light that filtered in between the wooden slats. Just a few minutes more and then we'd be in the city and able to sneak off the cart and away without Essena noticing.

I felt for Abghar's hand and he held mine tightly.

And then the cart started to move again. It turned a corner, shifting me into Abghar. He squeezed my hand tightly. The floor dropped out from under me so suddenly that I didn't have time to gasp. My brother wrapped me in a bearhug as we fell, rolling with me under and then over him and then leaping to his feet and dragging me to mine. We stumbled together into an alley mouth and looked out into the street.

My mouth dropped open. I'd been worried we'd be seen. The trap door opened up into two doors that dropped us neatly to the ground and I could still see them swinging under the cart as it turned a corner. The occupants hadn't noticed. Neither had the people of the city. And no wonder. This entire section was a ruin, ravaged by fires, still smoking. In some places, the embers still glowed in the ruined houses. The few people in the streets were soot-covered and picking through the rubble, heads down and shoulders drooping.

It felt like someone had slapped me in the face. This was not what Glorious Ingvar had looked like when I'd left. It was not the strong city of tales and legend.

"Come on," Abghar said in a low voice. "We have to cover a lot of ground to get in place by dusk."

I followed him down the alley, nodding when he put his fingers to his lips. There wasn't time for catching up, even now. We worked our way at a fast pace, moving slowly south and west. We didn't pass anything familiar to me, but anything I saw before would have been seen in the heat of battle and as I fled. And now, it would be seen from the eyes of someone trying to blend in with the knots of worried people, fear fresh and sharp in their eyes. The roll from the cart had actually helped with that, smearing us both with soot.

Every corner of the streets saw a patrol of Claws in blue uniforms embroidered heavily in white. They carried their swords naked, their eyes ever watchful. This time, no one fought back. No one lifted so much as their gaze. The city was beaten. Any move here would fail.

We passed a long line of people ending where a pair of monks were serving wooden bowls of soup and I edged closer to Abghar, speaking in an undertone.

"We can't do this. We should leave now. There's no one here left to fight with the Single Wing in this city."

"If we do that," he hissed back, "The Single Wing will see it as treachery. We agreed to come here and enact the plan. We must keep our word, or the rest of the family will suffer."

"Even if it accomplishes nothing?" I asked.

He nodded, a cynical twist to his mouth. "That's responsibility for you, Aella. Sometimes it means doing tasks that seem empty to keep the people you love fed and cared for. Sometimes it means doing things you know will hurt or demoralize you. But you do them because you love someone else more than your own happiness, more than your own fulfillment, more than your own life. It's those little sacrifices that bring honor. That little giving of yourself bit by bit for someone else. And the funny thing is that often doing that is the only way to truly find your own happiness. Most of the time, happiness is found in someone else's smile."

I shared one of those smiles with him and memories of my nieces' and nephews' small grins filled me up as we strode toward our empty mission. We could do this. And then we'd escape the city and go back to the ones we loved. Just like we promised.

We bought a bowl of soup at a stand when it was a few hours past midday and shared it together quickly. I thought that perhaps I was tired. I hadn't seen anything from my bees in a while. Or maybe there was nothing to report. Everyone would be getting into place just like we were.

I had my first vision when we finally reached the docks – just before dusk.

I stumbled as the vision flashed over me and Abghar gripped my arm. "Stay with me. What do you see?"

"Oska and Raquella at the docks," I whispered.

I could see them clear as day and yet I could still feel Abghar's hand on my arm and listen to his voice. Maybe I was getting better at this.

"They're with a group of other people. They're struggling to get to where they need to be. There are Claws off duty at the tavern they were supposed to meet at."

My vision snapped back, and I shuddered.

"Keep telling me when you see something," Abghar said calmly. "More information can only help us."

He held on to me as we made our way along these docks. Unlike the rest of the city, they were full to brimming with people – sailors in light-colored clothing, Claws in their bright jackets, dock workers looking clean in their soot-free clothing. Nothing had burned here.

The scent of brine and wet wood was almost pleasant after all that ash and I sucked it in greedily.

Out at anchor, at least twenty ships were bobbing on the waves. I couldn't stop to count them, but they seemed to be so many that I blinked at the sight, not sure if I was seeing what was really there.

I blinked again and another vision seized me. I gripped Abghar's arm and whispered as I watched.

"It's Alect. He's with Royn. They've met up with someone they know. A Claw. They're following him to the base of a tower."

"Good," Abghar murmured. His eyes were everywhere, watching the docks, but his hand wrapped over mine, leading me.

Another vision.

"I want it ready by tonight."

I froze and Abghar had to pull me to remind me to keep walking. I was looking out from Le Majest's belly over the slithering body of a spirit snake toward a large cage – big enough for a tiger.

"If I might ask, Le Majest, what do you hope to put in the cage?" I couldn't see the speaker, but he sounded rattled.

"A trophy," Juste sounded far too excited. I didn't want to know what – or who – he was planning that for.

I shuddered as Abghar eased me against the wooden slats of a low shed. "What did you see?"

"Le Majest. He is distracted by decorations."

"Good. Hopefully, he'll stay that way until we grab his attention."

Abghar ducked into a low doorway, pulling me with him and shutting the door behind him. Outside, the dock continued to bustle.

"Only two of you?" a voice in the darkness whispered.

It took a moment for my eyes to adjust as Abghar made his introductions. It was a fishmonger's shed. It had been cleaned after today's catch – but not well – and the smell of dead fish lingered in the air. But under a canvas were barrels of oil and the little grimy man who was waiting for us shoved a lantern in Abghar's hands.

"It's a shame to burn any more of the city. Even for the Single Wing."

"We need them distracted," Abghar said.

"I won't be with you when you do it," the small man said. "I thought I could be when they came to me but … I lost my boy in the fighting when the fools tried to take the city. I've lost too much. I don't want any more of this."

Abghar was nodding. "Can you get out without being seen?"

The man nodded. "Just make sure that when they catch you it isn't in here. I don't want anyone knowing it was me."

Abghar caught his arm. "We're not going to get caught."

"That's what they said when they attacked the Claws and tried to take the city. And now they're lined up in stocks, rotting and mostly dead. They kill them in groups of ten every hour and they've been doing it since that night. My sister Madrin was killed this morning. My old mother the day before that. They don't care how old or young you are. If they caught you on the streets that night, you're dead. Causes and hopes are all well and good but what does that do for my family? What does that do for me?"

Aghar sighed. "Maybe you should get out of the city."

"Where did you think I was going?" the man asked sourly. "I was here because I said I would be here. And now I am gone."

He was out of the little shed before I realized he was really going. Outside the sun was sinking low and I was rocked with another vision.

Retger and Zayana crouched in an alley outside a fine house.

"You're ready for this," he was whispering to her. "Stick to the plan. I'll be there with you."

"What if one of the real Wings is there?" she sounded like she'd asked that question more than once.

"Then they'll call our bluff, and we'll have to fight, but I don't think it will come to that."

He leaned in and I thought he was going to kiss her. I gasped and my vision faded.

"Retger is in place," I whispered.

Abghar nodded. "If only those fools had realized you were a resource and not a liability, we could have sat you in a room with Victore and you could have told us everything that was happening while he told us how to use that information."

"What now?" I asked.

"When the sun is fully set, we're going to start rolling out the barrels with the stoppers pulled out. It will look like we're just moving them, but it should pour oil down along the path. Once it's all poured out, we light it with the lantern, and then we run. It's a poor plan for a distraction, but they didn't send us out here to succeed. We'll have fulfilled our bargain and our family will be safe. You'll start with this barrel. Stay to the left of this shed when you roll it out and once it's empty just stand it up beside the nearest upright and then hurry back here."

I bit my lip. This all felt foolish to me. It felt like we were in the wrong place. It felt like the hammer was about to drop on us at any moment.

"Just hold on, little sister. I'll have us out of here before you know it," Abghar said in the darkness. I was glad it was too dark for him to see my face and all my doubts.

CHAPTER FIFTEEN

We rolled our barrels out onto the docks. The crowds were clearing slightly, but it was still busy. People scurried across the docks with goods in barrows or began to stow nets and traps in little sheds. Some smaller boats were rowing out to the ships at anchor laden with men returning from the city and others were rowing in with their hulls full of men and women coming in on leave. All of them seemed too busy to notice the hole in my barrel or that it was leaking oil.

The barrel grew lighter until I could tell it was almost empty and then I stood it up beside a lonely looking shed that smelled of fish and made my way back the way I'd come. I was just walking into the shed when a vision hit me and I lurched, stumbling into the stack of barrels.

"Wake up, wake up!" Helissa was saying, frantically shaking Osprey.

His beautiful eyes fluttered open, but my sister was fraught with worry. She shoved his swords at him.

"It's coming for us. If you can use these, get on your feet."

The bee shifted – brighter than usual – and I saw my family gathering the children together in the kitchen. Every sister and brother, sister-in-law or brother-in-law who had been left behind had a weapon in hand and a sack or a toddler or baby tied to their back.

What was happening? My breath came out in bursts.

"What's going on?" Abghar's voice was harsh, but I couldn't catch my breath or find my voice.

Wing Ivo hurried over to Osprey, coughing as he helped his friend up.

"Get your feet under you and your muscles will remember the rest," he said. "Help me, Victore."

The elderly general was there in a heartbeat, his ravens flying frantically around him.

"What's happening?" Osprey asked muzzily.

"We're under attack."

I blinked back to where Abghar watched me with anxiety all over his face.

"The children," I gasped. "Our family that we left behind – they're under attack."

"Who is attacking?" There was so much tension in his words – as much as I was feeling and more.

I shook my head. "I don't know. Helissa seemed worried."

"And Gabardeen?" he asked after his wife.

"She was holding a knife."

He cursed.

"You have to go back there," I said, grabbing his arm. "You need to leave now!"

He glanced at the barrels around me.

"I'll finish this," I said. "Without my recognizable face you can get back there fast. Steal a horse. Ride all the way."

He was staring at me, but I knew he was thinking about it. I rocked in place as a sudden burst of vision clouded my sight. Alect and Royn in the middle of a clash. Someone yelled in pain. Alect's face went white.

Then the vision faded and it was just Abghar and me again.

"Go. I will finish this job."

"And how will you escape again?" he asked breathlessly, his frizzled curls bouncing as he quivered with indecision.

"How were we planning to escape?"

"There would be a cart in the dye market with a spool of purple cloth hanging precariously from the back and the name "Cartsworth" painted on the side. We were to hide in that cart and the carter would drive out of the city with us."

"Then that's what I'll do," I assured him. "But someone needs to go save our family. They're under attack."

"They have the Wings and they're all strong and skilled." He was hesitating.

"The Wings are injured. The children can't fight on their own, and you know all the plans of the Single Wing and where to find help."

He couldn't argue with that. He didn't try. He just shook his head and made the sign of the bird.

"Get out of this alive or I will die of guilt," he whispered.

"Relentless," I replied, and then he was gone. By the time I had another barrel ready and was rolling it along the dock, I couldn't even see him in the crowd. This distraction was my responsibility now and I'd better make it good. The Single Wing was counting on it. And Abghar was counting on me.

I was fine until the third barrel and then the visions started coming too quickly. It was hard to go more than a few steps without being rocked by one. I was afraid to call the bees back – afraid to lose this vital lifeline but I couldn't fulfill this task and have them constantly distracting me.

"Can you simmer down a little, bees?" I whispered to myself as the bees showed me Retger sprinting across the cobblestones with Zayana at his back and then quickly shifted to show Alect again – this time white-faced, a bloody sword clutched in his hand. He was calling for help.

I swallowed down fear and brought out the next barrel and the next as I was rocked with visions of my family launching their attacks.

I was down to the last barrel when the vision overwhelmed me. Raquella was screaming as Oska turned back to her, hand spread out.

"Run!" he called, gritting his teeth and turning back to where a knot of men descended on him, swords flashing in the light of a nearby lantern. Raquella threw the lantern on a line of oil with a cry. Flames leapt up, dancing down the line of oil and bursting into orange and red curtains.

Oska screamed as a blade tore through him.

And then I was back in my own body again, gasping for breath, hoping beyond hope that I hadn't really seen that. I fell to my knees, dizzy suddenly.

Far too soon, another vision crashed over me.

Alect was on the top of the wall fighting alongside a fierce looking woman. Brielle! I thought she'd been banished by Le Majest. Perhaps the Single Wing had found her and recruited her. I felt a small stab of joy that she was alive at the same moment that a blade bit deep into her arm. She spun, curling in under her opponent's guard and slashing a backhand across his face before she was out of my view. Alect had his back to her, desperately knocking aside blows from two men on the wall who were pressing in on him. Behind them, more waited for their chance. Was it just the two of them back to back?

My heart raced in fear but there was nothing I could do to help. Nothing.

One of the Claws made a clever strike, slashing Alect's thigh. He fell to his knee with a moan and the second Claw rushed forward.

I forced all my fear and rage into the bee who was watching him, and she buzzed forward. The Claw slashing at Alect drew nearer and nearer as the bee – burning so bright I could barely look at it – rushed toward his eye. And then all I saw was a huge eye. And nothing. I felt heat and pain and then the bee was gone, and I was back in my own body leaning against the wall of a boathouse.

In the dusky twilight, no one had seen me slump here. Or if they had, they'd kept to their own business. In the darkness, someone laughed. I did not feel like laughing. My legs were like jelly as I wobbled back to the shed to retrieve the lantern. All I had to do was light the oil and get out of here and then I could go and help my family.

Knowing that they were out there in danger and in need made me feel like there was an ache between my shoulder blades.

I flew through the door of the shed and snatched up the

lantern, fumbling with the striker. It lit at last, filling the room with light. I lifted it up, looking for where the trail of oil was on the floor. It was right here somewhere. There!

I knelt down to light it.

And everything went black.

CHAPTER SIXTEEN

I woke up to a voice I'd hoped to never hear again.

"Awake again, wife? It seems that the owl is better than the Osprey when it comes to netting bees."

I gritted my teeth and opened my eyes. My head was pounding like a drum. I shut them immediately against the flooding pain.

I caught the barest glimpse of Juste Montpetit sitting on an ornate chair, one leg slung over the arm of the chair as he regarded me. He had a delicate hand lifted with a single finger resting against his chin and the fingers of the other hand twirled one of his large dark curls between his fingers. He was watching me with a predatory smile on his full lips.

Beside him Wing Essena stood, stroking her spirit owl nervously. It had diminished slightly. Was that worry in her eyes?

"You betrayed me," I whispered.

"You didn't really think you could outrun an owl, did you?" Essena asked, with ice in her tone. "I was watching you from his eyes in the sky. And you didn't even look up. Besides, what you call betrayal, I call patriotism. I love the Winged Empire and everything it stands for. Without it, we're nothing but barbarians clawing at the dust. With it, we are great – a nation capable of producing fine pottery, rippling cloth, tinkling music, and magic beyond what you settlers on a distant continent can ever dream of."

She flicked a finger toward a nearby dark window. The window frame had been carved with feathers and the drapes were woven in a pattern of red cranes on a white field. Beside the window, someone had placed a large, gilded vase, also patterned in cranes.

"Do you think any of that was made on this hard land of yours? You're nothing but what we brought here. You'll be nothing once we leave."

Juste made an irritated growling sound in his throat.

"We're done here," he said to her, snapping his fingers. "Leave."

"But Le Majest," she began, her face paling to grey.

His head swiveled like he was the owl – shock and fury on his face in equal portions.

"You dare to rise above your station and question me?" I heard the threat in his tone – and I heard it echoed in the feather in my breast as if it could sense things about him that I could not.

"But I brought you valuable information! I know the leadership of the rebels. I know how to find them. I found your wife and brought her here. I've been loyal to you. I –"

The spirit-snake shot out of his hand and tangled around her throat. She gagged.

"Where were you when I needed your blood to hold back the Forbidding?" he asked icily. "Where were you when my insides were exposed to the outside?" He motioned to the honeycomb in his belly. "Hiding. Preserving your own skin. Building your own empire. Do you think I don't realize that you've been playing both sides as you waited to find an opportunity for power in either of them? The information you have been sending Wing Xectare is nothing but useless dribbles. Enough to keep your hand in the game, but not enough to truly show your loyalty to me. You were waiting for a bargaining chip. And you found one. Returning my wife to me has bought you a second chance. Nothing more. Accept that it was all you were able to achieve."

She gasped as the snake slackened its hold. "Yes, Le Majest."

He smiled slightly. "Don't you think I might like to spend the night alone with my new wife?"

"Yes, Le Majest." She sounded like she'd used up all her breath.

"Then run along while you still have legs."

He retracted the snake and she scurried from the room as fast as her legs could carry her.

I took the opportunity to examine the bone-white bars encircling me. There was enough room for me to lie down fully stretched out and not a hair more. There was enough room to stand – maybe even put another one of me sitting on my shoulders. As cages went, it was generous in size.

But it was still a cage. And I saw no door in it.

"I had it made just for you, wife. Consider it a wedding present. I even had them craft bees to decorate it."

My eyes snapped to him and I carefully pulled myself to my feet. I felt the back of my head. It was sticky with blood. Essena must have hit me from behind. The thought of that made my bees buzz with fury, filling me with the warmth of their rage.

"There," Juste said, smiling, his lips parting slightly as if he were savoring the moment. "That's exactly the lovely fury I've come to expect from my wife."

"I'm not your wife," I said, poison dripping from my words, but the feather in my chest had dulled to a happy warmth, glowing and contented rather than furious. I looked around the cage for any kind of weapon or way of escape. The cage had no lock. No door. They must have welded the bars in place around me. I felt ill at the thought.

My fingers drifted to the cuff around my wrist, reaching inside. The feather there was stone cold.

The cage was positioned in what must be Juste's makeshift throne room. It was large with more than one balcony wide open showing the smoldering embers of Glorious Ingvar through the windows.

"I see you like what I've done with the place," he said languidly. "So do I. Smoke has always suited me. It curls and loops just like a snake."

He sighed, looking into the distance with his huge blue eyes. The finger on his chin traveled up to his lips and he bit it before speaking again.

"You have to stop running from me, wife. You're meant to be by my side."

"I told you that I'm not –"

He lunged before I could finish the sentence. He was on his feet, his arms snaking through the bars and grabbing a handful of my hair. He yanked me hard so that I crashed against the bars and with his other hand he opened my shirt and revealed the feather on my collarbone.

"You can't deny it when my marker is in you. You are mine,

Aella of House Shrike. I agreed to keep you close and I have. I have honored you and you try to deny it."

I gasped and channeled all my fury into my bees. They flowed from me, swirling around us both. I tried to ask them to lift the cage. Please try, I thought. Please try.

I was searching for my other bees in my mind – for any clue of how things had gone for my siblings – Oska who had been stabbed, Alect with that slash to his leg, Abghar who must have reached the rest by now. Osprey… any of them. I saw nothing.

"I made sure there were no locks that bees could open this time. They can't help you now. They can only sting, and I don't mind your little stings. They remind me I'm alive."

"My bees do more than sting. They're what patched you up."

He ignored my jab.

"I felt it the moment that my brother was no longer tied to me," Juste said, hissing in my face. His snake materialized around his shoulders and then slid out around mine, tugging me closer to him. I tried to fight it, pushing and shoving at the snake, my breath coming too fast as I fought, but I couldn't budge those spirit coils. "Did you know that by cutting the tie you have elevated me? That was you wasn't it? I thought I smelled honey."

"What do you want me to say?" I asked through gritted teeth.

"I want you to prove to me what the Hissan said – that you are useful and should be kept close."

"And why would I do that?"

He tilted his head and smiled slightly.

"Because if you don't, I'll kill your brother." He nodded his head and the Claw beside the door opened it. Two others dragged in a slumped figure. Blood trailed behind him leaving a red streak on the white marble floor. "After all, you took mine. It's only fitting that I take yours."

"Abghar," I gasped.

He twitched as if he was trying to move his head but stayed slumped between the Claws. I couldn't see his face – couldn't see if he was so badly beaten that he couldn't survive.

Panic welled up inside me, making my breathing turn raw and harsh. They'd found him somehow. And they'd beaten him.

"Now, be a good girl and do something useful – tell me something to show me that you know more than what is right before your eyes. Give me some kind of insight into what that snake showed you."

"I saw trails that lead underground."

His eyes grew dark and he spat to the side. "I said something valuable. I have no need of trails under the ground."

There was nothing I had learned from the Hissan that could help him. Not that I knew of. I paused, trying to think and he nodded to the Claws. One of them slugged Abghar in the torso and he groaned.

"Wait! Stop."

"Tell me something interesting and they will stop."

"I watched Ixtap slay the Emperor." The words seemed to tumble out but now I had his full attention. He lifted a hand to stop his Claws from striking again and gazed into my eyes. "He strode into the throne room and claimed the Winged Empire in your name. This morning."

"So soon," he whispered, but he sounded pleased. "So soon, and it is already done. But I feel nothing."

His hand reached up to his chest where his shirt surely held his own feather. He pursed his lips, thinking, and then seemed to notice Abghar suddenly. He flicked a finger.

"Take that thing away."

"No," I pled, "please, he's so hurt."

Tears filled my eyes and Juste smiled. "You took my brother from me without letting me say a proper goodbye. It's only fair that the same should happen to you, don't you think?"

"Please."

"Tell me, did he forgive you when he lay dying? Did he call you brave for cutting out his feather? I could have warned you that trying to free him would kill him. It was one of the little traps my father laid in that bond. But I think I will be more sorry that you killed him than you will. After all, you got to marry the real prince. You get to be the real empress."

"Please." Abghar's blood was making a trail across the white marble floor.

"We'll need to make you ready for the coronation."

The Claws were nearly to the door.

"Abghar," I called, my voice trembling. "I love you."

He gasped, but he didn't speak, and I still couldn't see his face. I willed my bees – my useless bees – to go with him and heal him but I couldn't tell if they'd obeyed. My eyes were blurry with tears and my swarm buzzed uselessly around me, unable to bring me out of the cage or defend me in any way.

"I will send a dress for you to wear," Juste said, releasing his grip on me. The snake slithered from my shoulders and back to his. It tangled around his shoulders and neck like a scarf. "When it arrives, you will wear it, or your brother will know true pain."

He struck a dramatic pose as he watched me, as if I was a mirror he was looking into and not a person.

"You don't need him." I'd been so strong standing up to Juste before. So why did I feel so weak now? Why did I feel as if my knees were about to buckle?

"He's a dangerous rebel," Juste said, watching me as if looking for a reaction. "Someone Wing Essena calls 'the Single Wing.' She says they bear tattoos – which should make them easy to find. It's one of the few good pieces of information that she offered. I already have my Claws scouring the population for the markings. Executions will begin tomorrow. Be sure you're dressed for them."

He strode toward the door and then stopped.

"Oh. I forgot," he turned back and strode to my cage, carefully flicking a piece of lint off his jacket as if he wasn't even paying attention to me.

I tried to back up to the other side of the cage, but he flicked two fingers out and his snake spiraled toward me. It grabbed me tightly around the waist and dragged me forward as my feet slid across the floor of the cage.

"It's better not to fight it," he said, his eyes cold and hard. As soon as I was close, he reached for me. I knocked his hand aside, but the snake struck fast – coiling round and round me until my arms couldn't move.

He shook his head. "I don't know why you bother. It's a waste of energy."

He ripped my jacket aside, revealing my feather, and laid a hand over it. I gritted my teeth at his unwanted touch. Something pulsed over my heart and his snake seemed stronger somehow.

"I could get used to that," he said slipping his hand away. His snake disappeared and I gasped, clutching the bars for support and baring my teeth at him. "The marriage binding gives me access to some of your strength. Which should help with the insect problem."

I realized, blearily, that my bees had winked out – all but one of them.

He spun on his heel and strode out of the room and his guards went with him, leaving me alone in the cage.

CHAPTER SEVENTEEN

I slumped to the floor of the cage, all my injuries from the last days and weeks crashing in on me as if it had been the bees that had dulled their edge and sped their healing. Maybe it had been. I could feel where I'd been stabbed by Osprey in that snake cathedral when he'd sprung to Juste's defense. It hurt like it had ripped open again, but when I slid my jacket aside, the skin was healing just as before. Perhaps, I'd never felt the full pain of it until now.

"Can you do that, little bee?" I whispered to the one sad, lone bee who landed beside me on the cage floor. "Have you been taking my pain and speeding my healing?"

The places where I'd been beaten by Juste's guards ached now to the point where it hurt to move. So did the ankle I'd twisted as I ran through Karkatua and a slash in the skin of my arm. I couldn't even remember where I'd gotten that.

My head was swimming with so much pain that I leaned over and let myself fall to the cage floor, feeling a little relief at the cold of the metal against my aching head. I wanted to lie here and cry. I wanted to give up. But I didn't dare. There had to be some way out. There just had to be. And then I'd find my brother and get him out, too.

I closed my eyes – just for a moment. I still needed to put that dress on, so they didn't hurt Abghar. Darkness – a welcome escape – flooded over me and I clung to it, wishing I knew what to do next. I had to escape if I was going to help anyone, and yet I could hardly seem to lift my own head.

A vision buzzed into my head – fainter than usual so that I couldn't make out fine details. It was Alect. He had a nasty cut on his cheek. Blood flowed down his face. My heart lurched at the sight of it – but his face was alight with joy. His hand formed a fist, clutched above his head. My bee started to pull back and drift upward and I could see he was on top of a tower. Beside him, a Claw I didn't recognize threw off his blue jacket, tossing it over the side of the tower. He reached for the banners hanging from the tower's edge – banners showing the white swan of the Imperial House. He began to slice them neatly so that they fell to the ground. They'd won.

The bee drew a little higher still and that's when I saw Royn's body slumped at the top of the stairs. Dead or alive? I wondered, and then my bee went dark.

I blinked my eyes open and saw there were two bees in front of me on the cage floor – as if one had somehow transported right from one place to the other. But that made no sense. I was delirious. That was all. Broken by pain and exhaustion.

The bees began a strange circling dance.

I closed my eyes again.

When the next vision came, it startled me out of sleep, so that I didn't know if I was dreaming or seeing something.

Retger stood on the top of a wide staircase, face tight with some emotion I couldn't read. He looked deeply troubled, but he raised his voice as he looked out over a crowd of people.

"Citizens of Portua Town. The Single Wing has taken your

city on behalf of all men and women who wish freedom from the Winged Empire. We are taking all of Far Stones. If your allegiance is still to the Winged Empire, you may make your way to the docks before nightfall tomorrow and every person who requests passage will be loaded on the ships there to return to the continent. You have our word. It's more of a chance than you ever gave us."

He blinked back tears, his face contorting for a moment before he continued.

"I have just come from the cellars of this house. I have seen what was done to the people here who spoke their minds. Who kept weapons to defend their families and were caught. Who wanted freedom. We will not treat you in such a barbarous way. But we will remember."

"Far Stones!" Someone in the crowd called and the cheer was taken up. Retger made the sign of the bird, but he looked exhausted – wrung out by what he'd seen.

Out of nowhere, a dark shape surged from a pillar at the side of the entrance, a knife in his hand. I cried out a warning, but Retger couldn't hear me. The man was closer, closer – I wanted to shut my eyes, but I didn't dare look away, my breath caught in my lungs. Notice him! Notice him!

Scarlet seared across my vision and Flame burst between Retger and the man with the knife. Retger stumbled, falling to one knee and my heart lurched again. Flame extended his claws, and the spirit-bird shoved the attacker back, screeching as he attacked. He had grown again. He was nearly the size of an eagle. Zayana stepped out from where she'd been standing in the crowd, arms crossed and fury on her usually calm face.

"This Wing stands with Far Stones. This spirit bird stands with

Retger of House Shrike."

As if to punctuate her words, the bird lunged, pecking at the attacker's eyes and driving him to his knees. There was a scuffling sound and then people were surging onto the spot, surrounding the would-be assassin and looking to Zayana who lifted a hand to Flame. He shot back up in the air, circling her protectively as she stood beside Retger.

"I saw a sign today – two beetles fighting on a stone. The smaller beetle ate the head of the larger beetle. So, it is with the Far Stones. We will eat the head of the Winged Empire."

My mind was spinning so much that I almost wondered if these signs she saw actually meant something.

Retger surged to his feet. "Stand with us! Stand for Far Stones!"

And then my vision winked out and I blinked awake again. I now had three bees doing their strange dance before me. And their dance had morphed into something agitated. What in the world were they doing?

I managed to lift my head – finally – and I twisted to get my arms under me and push me up to all fours. I had to pause there to catch my breath, wincing in pain from all my injuries. They stole my breath away. I took in long, slow gasps of air for a minute, and then I eased myself into a sitting position. There was one thing I could do to help my family right now. I could put on this dress.

Changing my clothes was an agonizingly slow process that left me sweaty and gasping. When I was done, I slumped back on the floor, my head cradled on the ball of clothing I'd been wearing.

The dress that Juste had provided was a gossamer golden

creation with a high lace neck and puff-topped court sleeves that ended in lace points over my hands. The skirt was full enough for movement but narrow in profile. It looked like a wedding dress. The thought that it might very well be one, turned my stomach.

At least Abghar wouldn't be beaten for my disobedience. I'd managed that much. My boots, I kept. I also kept my belt and short sword in the scabbard. Oddly, my captors hadn't bothered to take it from me. Perhaps they thought I couldn't do anything with it anyway. There was no point in declawing a dead cat.

I stared at the sword for a long time, wondering what I should do. I had a few options, even in a cage.

I could try to draw the sword and kill Juste the next time he was close, but he was wary enough that I'd be unlikely to get the opportunity. After all, he had only come close to me when his snake had me in its grasp.

I could fall on this sword and take my life. I did not want to do that. My mind shied away from even considering it beyond just listing it. I desperately wanted to see how everything turned out and I still couldn't shake the hope that somehow, we could survive all this – that we could succeed.

I already knew that Alect and the Single Wing had succeeded at the towers, seizing at least one of them. I knew that Retger and the Single Wing had successfully taken Portua Town. But what about the rest? What would happen? Could we win? There were too many questions that made me long for answers.

I could also use the sword to stab myself in the chest and send one of my bees in to burn out the Forbidding in me and rescue me from my tie to Juste. I could do that. My hands shook at the thought of harming myself and I wondered if my magic would operate with me only half-conscious – or unconscious. There would be no friend to nurse me or help me get to safety. There would be no one to make sure I didn't die from it. I wasn't sure if I had the guts to try or not. And in either case, I didn't have the energy just yet.

I closed my eyes and drifted off. When I next woke, I blinked myself awake before the vision caught me.

"There's still fighting in the port district and we couldn't stop riders from escaping to the East. There have been pigeons released, too. By now, Glorious Ingvar will know we've tried to take the city," Oska was telling an older man who was frowning over the plans laid out before him. "We need General Victore. We left him at the hidden location before we set out, but I could go retrieve him."

"We almost have the city," the older man said. He'd tattooed the wing right on his cheek in a flagrant display of his loyalties. It still looked fresh. "By the end of another day, we'll have it."

"And then Le Majest will send his troops against us. He has half the Imperial Claws of the Winged Empire with him since those ships arrived. We are not ready to defend Karkatua when we haven't even secured it yet." Oska shot a helpless glance to Raquella. "At least with General Victore we have a chance of surprising them with a strategy they won't expect. He used to be one of them. He knows how they work in a way we simply don't."

"Don't underestimate me, boy," the older man said. "You and your house have been invaluable, but you are not your father. When I came over on the boats with him, we made sacrifices you'll never understand."

"If you mean killing your own people to hold back the Forbidding," Oska said in a low tone, "then you're right. I won't ever understand it."

"I can go," Raquella said quietly as the two of them faced off, their expressions darkened with matching fury. "I know the way back. I can go and get Victore and return with him."

The older man shook his head. "Go, then. At least it will get your brother off my back."

My bee hovered, drifting from Oska to Raquella and back again. Oh. It needed to decide who to follow. Would it take input from me? And who should I choose? I felt suddenly anxious. Raquella was likely walking into a trap. Oska was still fighting in the city. Who did I need to see? Who did I need to watch?

"Go with Raquella," I whispered. "Help guide her so she avoids the trap."

It was magic – so I shouldn't have been surprised, and yet I was still stunned when the bee buzzed to my sister and landed on her head as she hugged Oska goodbye.

"Hurry," he whispered, and then my vision evaporated.

My heart was racing, racing, racing and I couldn't seem to catch my breath. The door to the room opened and two men dressed in Imperial livery came in with a pair of Claws.

The men in livery were carrying a tray and a bundle of cloth.

"Put the chamber pot in front of the slot and stand to the back of the cage," one of the Claws said.

I hadn't used the chamber pot and I didn't have the strength to move it. I tottered to my feet and stumbled away from them and one of the men in livery sniffed with disdain and shoved the tray in his hands through a small slot at the bottom of the cage on that side. It would have been just wide enough for my arm to reach out. He stepped back smartly – careful to stay out of my reach if I were to make a sudden lunge, clear the entire cage, and reach out through it to him.

I almost rolled my eyes, but I was too excited by the smell of tea in a saucer and toasted bread with butter. My stomach growled.

"If you do not need the chamber pot emptied, then at least shove your old clothing through the slot," the man in livery ordered.

I didn't move. I didn't want to lose my clothing. Osprey had given me that jacket. It was precious to me. And there were no pockets in the dress. Nowhere for my flint or coins.

He sighed and rolled his eyes. "If you will not allow us to wash your clothing then you will at least accept this leather bag." He took the bag from on top of the stack of things in the other man's arms. "Move the tray and I will push it in through the slot. Please put your things in it so you are tidy for the coming ceremony. There is a bowl of water with your tea. You may use it to wash yourself and make yourself presentable. We will come back for the dishes."

I stumbled forward and bent painfully down to pull the tray aside. The man in livery waited until I was back on the other side of the cage, nursing the tea in my hands. He shoved the bag through the bars quickly and scurried away. The other servant set down the bundle of cloth and hurried away with him and to my horror, the Claws lifted the cloth and deftly began to cover the cage as if I was a bird being covered for the night.

My lip curled in irritation, but what could I do? Humiliated, I ate my toasted bread and tea and tried very hard not to feel like the animal they were treating me as.

It would be okay. It really would. My family was succeeding in fighting back. Half of Far Stones was in the hands of the Single Wing after just one night of attacks. They could win.

But I was worried. I hadn't seen a glimpse of Osprey or the children since that last vision and I didn't know if they were safe, or in mortal peril, or … I didn't dare think of what the last option might be.

I finished eating, cleaned my face with the water, and tried to untangle my hair with my fingers, but it was no use. I was exhausted and in agony. Was it just that my bees had propped me up for so long and now they were gone, or had the Prince taken something more from me? Something I couldn't get back?

Carefully, I undid the top of my dress and drew the short sword from my scabbard. My hands were shaking badly. I'd never physically harmed myself before and I didn't want to do it now, either. I knew well enough how youth and strength were gifts. All too soon they would be taken away. But what else could I do? He was going to drain me dry with this feather if I left it here.

Carefully, I lined the blade up with the feather. I just needed to pierce it. It didn't need to be very deep. But a sword – even a short one – is not a knife. It was too unwieldy for such a delicate task. I sat on the floor, bracing the hilt between my feet, and used my palms along the flat of the blade to guide the sharp tip in place. Do it, Aella. Do it.

I leaned into the sword, forcing myself to lean past the pain, but not too far past. I gasped in agony as it pierced the skin, crying out despite myself. Was the cut deep enough? I pulled myself back and the sword clattered to the ground as my shaking hand reached up to touch the wound. It was deep. My hand came away slick with blood.

"Please, bees. Please go in there and cut me free! Please burn away the roots of Forbidding in me and purify me of their tangle. Set me free, set me free."

I didn't know if they heard me – if they even could. I passed out from the pain.

I woke to someone slipping my tray out of the cage. The moment my eyes flickered open he squeaked and then the cover fell back down on the cage and he fled.

"Dead! She's dead! She's killed herself!" He was screaming as he ran.

I moaned and pulled myself up, finding my old shirt in the leather bag and using it to staunch the blood and wipe up what I could from my chest and hands. There was just so much. Too much.

And I didn't feel my bee inside the wound. The bees – the three of them – were still dancing their frantic dance beside me as if there were nothing else in all the world to do.

I passed out again.

Chapter Eighteen

I woke up to his eyes on mine and I tried to scream but my mouth was gagged by a coil of snake.

"What have you done, wife?" Juste asked coolly. "Did you think you could use your magic on yourself?" He rolled his eyes as if I was a foolish child and not a grown woman. "If you'd studied for more than a handful of days under a proper Wing, they could have told you that no one can use their magic on their own bodies. A Wing cannot tear themselves to shreds with their own bird. I cannot strangle my own life out with my snakes, and you cannot fill yourself with wicked honeycomb as you filled me."

I said nothing. There was a snake blocking the chance of saying anything. I made sure he could see how I felt with the intensity of my gaze. My eyes crossed for just a moment and I almost thought I could see a glimmer of Osprey's face but then the image was gone, and I was back, looking at Juste.

"We're about to be coronated and you're a mess," he hissed. And I realized – in utter shock – that he was bandaging the wound on my chest with gentle hands.

I froze as his hands lifted the neck of my dress back in place, sliding around me to button the high collar up the back again.

"It will have to work – bloodstains and all," he said huskily. "I have no time to commission another."

He'd commissioned this?

"It matches my jacket, you'll note." And it did. He wore a dull gold jacket embroidered with black snakes. "Now that I will be emperor, I am doing away with Imperial blues and swans. I will no longer be of House Swan but of House Adder. And with my new reign, there will be a new era."

The snake slid from my face and I drew in a deep, shuddering breath, flexing against his hold on the rest of my body. Juste was leaning over me, one hand on either side of me pressed flat against the cage floor, his lovely face just inches from mine. The look in his eyes terrified me.

I opened my mouth to speak and to my shock, he kissed me. I froze and then bit down hard on his unwanted kiss.

He drew back, huffed a laugh, and then wiped the blood from his lower lip with his sleeve.

"And now we match, wife. Both wearing gold, trimmed in bloodstains. How considerate of you to add to my attire."

I wanted to be furious – and of course I was – but it was hard to feel the heat of fury beneath the icy cold fingers of terror that held my heart.

"And now we must be crowned. Which means leaving this cage. I've decided to leave your sword and your scabbard in place. Having you armed by my side will lead people to believe you are there willingly – but you will have no option but to come as I call and do as I say."

I gasped as his snake seemed to pulse and then it was standing me up, sliding down from the upper half of me and ducking beneath my skirts. I clenched my teeth, kicking hard against the gripping coils, but there was no stopping the snake as it came to rest at mid-thigh under the sweeping skirt. It rippled along my legs and as I shuddered again at its embrace. It moved me forward, gliding behind Juste who stepped out of a door cut into the cage.

My hands were tied tightly behind my back – with what I did not know, but I hoped it was not another snake.

"Our glorious reign awaits us, Aella of House Shrike. You are honored to be at my side. Together, we stand for love and peace in the Empire."

"The kind of love that murdered your father?" I shot back. I was powerless to stop the snake as it kept drawing me forward, forward, forward behind Juste.

"I have always exemplified the best of loves. It is only those full of hate who oppose me," Juste said calmly, but he looked over his shoulder at me and his eyes flickered with madness.

"The kind of peace that cuts out tongues and kills people a dozen at a time in the city streets?"

He made a moue with his mouth and shook his head. "It is so hard to expunge hate from the hearts of the kinds of people who would oppose us – oppose me. I find it distasteful."

"But not so distasteful that you stop."

He leaned in close, grabbed me by the hair, and pulled me so I was inches from his nose.

"I can keep talking about this all day with you, but I am reminded you have a brother in my care who still draws breath. Perhaps you should remember that, too."

Abghar.

I shut my mouth with a click.

"Good girl. I knew marriage to you would be well worth it. Now, concentrate and see if you can conjure up a vision for me of what my allies are doing on the continent. We received the official message by bird this morning proclaiming the death of the emperor and the need to immediately coronate me, but it was brief to the extreme. Concentrate."

And despite myself and my horror at this situation, I did concentrate. I focused as hard as I could on my bees. Could I force a vision? Could any of them hear me?

I was led – though I hardly noticed in all my concentration – through the governor's manor and out to a waiting open-topped carriage. The snake deposited me in the seat facing Juste and he sat, carefully arranging himself to be seen best in the carriage. Still, I focused.

I concentrated on the bees as we rode through the streets to the cheers of the gathered crowds. And if those cheers were forced and anxious, and if they were backed up by Claws with drawn blades in their hands, then the people were no more unwilling than I was.

"Perhaps you should cut my bonds and let me draw from your feather as you drew from mine," I suggested when I could draw no vision from the air.

Juste regarded me for a very long time before simply saying, "No."

It was long minutes before he added, "But if you do not find something for me by the time we reach the coronation, I will kill your brother before your eyes. As a coronation present. Perhaps his death will concentrate your blood properly and you'll see what you need to see."

I closed my eyes and focused inward and my pleading with the bees turned into a prayer.

Flight of wind protect me, mercy of the skies fly over me, give me peace and protection, let me soar from this terror on the wings of eagles. Bridge the gap between my bee and me. Help me to reach his sight. Spare my brother. Spare him from death.

I gasped as my mind filled with a vision. It had worked!

The bee buzzed over Ixtap's shoulder and he tried to swat it away. My vision spun as the bee fell and then bobbed back up, circling violently to avoid the attacks of anyone in arm range. He settled – finally – further away than I would have liked. It took all my concentration to line up Ixtap's words with his lips. He was talking to a group of men and women who were dressed in clothing a little fancier than the Claws – their weapons inlaid with silver, their hair carefully coiffed, their clothing of a higher caliber, but it was still blue with swans stitched in white across the breasts and marching up the arms. Soon, if Juste had his way, it would be black and gold.

"Any resistance to the coronation of Le Majest, Juste Montpetit, is to be met with deadly force. When Le Majest arrives again on the shores of the Winged Empire, he should be received by only those who wish him a long and mighty reign."

"My Lord Ixtap," one of the men said, "we want the same things you do – a peaceful nation and Le Majest on the throne – but those who fight against this are like brothers to us. Surely there is a more peaceful way to end this fighting. Surely there is some way that does not include bloodshed."

"Surely?" Ixtap's voice was a warning. "Are you suggesting that the rebels have a right to raise banners and houses against us? Or to do so without retaliation?"

"Well – " The man was dark-haired and he wore a short coat sewn all over with yellow canaries.

"It is on the orders of Le Majest that we fight and claim his home for him. I repeat again, any man or woman found to stand against such orders will be cut down where they stand – they and their families."

"It will not be easy, Lord Surrogate," another one of the men said. He was older and had a lined face and worried expression with wings of white in his hair. He adjusted his goose-feather collar with a nervous hand. "Those who oppose this are strong in number. They represent nearly half of the Empire – certainly all the outlying islands. They wish for another manner in which to raise an emperor."

"Other than inheritance?" Ixtap asked with a raised brow.

"Yes, Lord Surrogate."

"Other than marriage as decreed by the law?"

"Yes, Lord Surrogate."

Wait, was his marriage to me also to make his reign look more legitimate?

"Other than great reputation in building the Empire and quelling rebellions?" Ixtap asked in nearly a whisper.

"No, Lord Surrogate."

"Then find me every one of them and we will begin executions at dawn. Start in House Osprey. I already dislike that place."

"But Lord Surrogate! That is the home of General Petren, a long-time ally of Le Majest. He has already openly declared his support for the new emperor." The older man's distress was echoed on the other faces around him.

"Has he? I'm sure there can still be some found in his household who must be quelled."

The man speaking paled and fell silent.

"I promised Le Majest an empire quelled and ready when he returns and I plan to offer it up to him," Ixtap said.

"That may be more difficult than you think, Lord Surrogate. This strange dark magic continues to be a problem. Even without Houses in rebellion, we would have to find some way to drive it back. Every night it swallows fields and hills faster than we can withdraw from its path. Unless a solution is found, we will lose our empire to –

"Silence!" Ixtap bellowed and with a snap, my vision released me.

"See something good?" Juste asked, eyes narrowed when I opened my eyes again.

"Yes," I said through gritted teeth.

"Something that might spare your brother's life?" he asked, one of his eyebrows lifting.

"I want him released," I said through gritted teeth. "I want him released or I tell you nothing."

Ixtap clicked his tongue. "Now why would I do that? I am already prepared to spare his life for this information, and you want more from me?"

"Am I not your wife?" I challenged, still gritting my teeth at the thought of that. "Is not everything you own mine as well?"

He snorted. "You have that backward. Everything you own is

mine. And look, the coronation stage is just ahead."

He was right. Ahead of us, people had been very busy. They had set the stage up in a wide spot in the street framed by one of the gates into the city. Seating was arranged on either side of the gate. On one side, the crowd was spread on the road outside the city and spreading across the fields. On the other side, the people were lining the streets and watching from the roofs of the nearby buildings.

The early morning sun poured through this eastern gate, and it would bathe Juste in light from one direction and leave him a dazzling silhouette from the other. Very dramatic. And so very him.

An arch had been arranged and hung with massive white gardenias as if this was a wedding rather than a coronation. A throne had been set under the arch, glowing brightly as the sun flared off its gilding. Someone must have been up all night to create that piece. He couldn't possibly have commissioned it before he heard from me that his father was dead … could he?

Juste leaned forward in his seat so he could whisper in my ear. His pose made it look like he was whispering an endearment, but his words belied the idea.

"Tell me what you saw before we reach the platform or the first thing you will see as Empress will be your brother's corpse."

CHAPTER NINETEEN

"Ixtap and those loyal to you are fighting over the Winged Empire with those who will not concede," I said, rushing to get it out.

"Who would not concede?" his eyes narrowed on me.

"I don't know," I said, shaking my head. "But the Forbidding is there, too. It somehow has crossed the sea and is taking homes and lands on the other side of the ocean."

He began to shake his head at me, but my vision was ripped violently away.

In my mind, I was finally seeing the person I wanted to see most, but this was not how I wanted to see him.

Osprey was fighting a tangle of Forbidding, sword in hand, dripping with sweat. Beside him, Adigale was trying to counter an attack to their left, but one of her arms hung uselessly to the side, swollen and purple in a way that turned my stomach. Anfrea was on his other side, swaying with exhaustion as she fought. And behind them, Os was spread wide. Under his glowing purplish-white wings, my nieces and nephews clung to one another, terror in their eyes as the great spirit-bird held back the Forbidding.

What had happened to them? And where were Wing Ivo and Victore? And Helissa? And all the others who were meant to be there with them?

A stab of cold shot through me and panic bubbled up. How long could they keep going like that? Where were they, even? I didn't know, and there was so little I could do for them, so little I could do to help. I felt the tears beginning to fall and I sucked in a sobbing breath.

"Please," I begged my bee inside my mind. "Please guide them out, somehow. Please show them the way to safety."

Would it have the strength to help? I felt so weak, and they needed me to sustain them.

Osprey's blue eye looked directly at my bee and I felt it flare brighter for a moment. Osprey's eyes seemed to soften for a brief second and then my vision was gone, and I was back in my body, tasting blood from where I'd bit my tongue.

It took me a moment to realize I was shaking from head to foot and when I did, I looked up into Juste's eyes. His eyes narrowed and his face looked smug.

"Anything that displeases you so can only be good for me. But turn your mind back to what I need, because, after the coronation, you need to concentrate very hard for me. The Hissan say that they gave you a memory in their snake temple – one meant only for the Adder. And that memory is the key for taking not just the Winged Empire but the whole world. You must dig out that memory – lost even to them – or we will have to do whatever we must to jar it loose."

If I hadn't already felt like my stomach was being wrung out like a dirty rag inside me, and my heart frozen to agonized ice, his words would have made me ill. But how could anything make me feel worse than I already felt?

Juste smiled at me nastily. "A little reminder of why you need to comply. You have a big family. I can find them all. We can take our time going through them one by one until you give me what I need."

He flicked his eyes to the side, and I saw a gallows had been set up on a street parallel to the one our carriage was taking to the dais. Hanging on the gallows was a man wearing the clothes I'd last seen Abghar in. He was the right size. The right shape. The right color.

I leaned over the side of the carriage and vomited to the shrieking horror of the crowd closing in on our carriage.

Juste flung a lace handkerchief at me but there was no pity in his eyes.

"Clean yourself. You have a crown to wear and a memory to find. The more time you spend worrying and thinking about your petty little family of rebels and criminals, the more time it will take to find that memory and that will only mean that more of them have to come here and face that fate." His face was cold as if none of this mattered to him and maybe it didn't. After all, hadn't he just killed his own father? Or at least ordered it done? "Don't forget. I know where they are. Every last one of them. The Owl proved to be at least some use to me after all."

The owl. Wing Essena. I'd been so horrified by her betrayal of Abghar and me that I hadn't stopped to think about all the other people she would betray – every member of the Single Wing out there including my family members.

I swayed, sickened and shaken, as the memory of Os crouching over the little children filled my mind. Where had everyone else been? Had they died fighting to save the little ones?

I couldn't focus anymore. Not on the cheering crowds, not on Juste's expression of triumph, not even on my own fear. My breath was speeding and speeding, and I couldn't stop the spiral of panic and sorrow that had caught me up like a whirlwind. It whipped my heart higher and higher, leaping above conscious thought into a spiraling storm of pain. Waves of nausea and clawing panic washed over me until I felt like I was choking on my own breath.

At some point, Juste snatched my cold hand in his clammy one. At some point, the snake stood me up and propelled me out of the carriage with him. It was all just sensations to me – isolated little horrors that meant nothing after the horrors I'd just witnessed. Oh, Abghar. Your death was my fault. Oh, my family, your fates are because of me.

Claws lined our path, their uniforms neat, their faces noble, their weapons gleaming. I wanted to knock them down like a line of wooden toys and watch them topple over each other. I wanted to scream and call my bees and fly out of there like a cloud. And yet, I couldn't do any of it. I was helpless before them as if I had no magic at all. Even the last three bees I had only sat on my shoulder, tired and lifeless.

Tears blinded me as we swept ahead of the carriage and Juste made a flourish with his hand to the crowd around us.

"Le Majest!"

"The Winged Empire!"

Even had I wanted to listen to their shouts and accolades, I would not have been able to. The snake carried me along as I fell into a vision.

Ixtap was reading a message. He tilted his head to the side. I could just read it through the bee's eyes over his shoulder.

Petren and House Osprey are missing. Rumor is, they took a ship.

He growled and picked up the next small message holder, opening it with a pinch of his fingers and slipping the delicate message out.

My vision flashed back to where we were, and I shook my head trying to clear it. We were at the edge of the dais.

"My snake must leave you now, wife," Juste said through his teeth. "Your hands will remain tied, but I'll hold you upright. Just don't miss any memory of the Hissan. I need those memories."

I gritted my teeth and tried not to flinch at his touch as he drew me to him. My feet felt clumsy after being slid along by a snake all the way here. I tottered up the steps to the dais and a voice above us rang out.

"Gather together, O my people! Gather together and be still before Le Majest!"

The crowd hushed and a choir began to chant a wordless song – one that carried majesty and dignity with every note – and the speaker intoned that poem I'd heard first from the mouth of Wing Ivo.

"Slither, scale, bend, squeeze,

The dark tangles the land,

The blood of the brave freeze,

New conquerors come on the sand."

We climbed the steps very slowly, Juste taking his sweet time as he drew every eye to himself. My eyes were glued to the horizon beyond the dais as I tried not to be ill. Which is how I noticed how close the Forbidding had crept to the road where the people were assembled – how it was creeping closer yet.

My vision swam and I tottered, this whole thing becoming like a waking dream. My gaze skittered up to the speaker. She was draped in strings of pearls that made it look like she had wings of pearl strings and a veil over the lower half of her face made entirely of pearls.

The speaker was still reciting:

"Soar, swoop, fly free,

The bird dives to the land,

The wing crosses the sea,

The bright leaves a brand."

We cleared the last step and Juste arranged us in front of the throne, his hand still on my upper arm. I wondered if the people noticed I was tied or that he was holding me against my will. There were a lot of things those loyal to the crown chose not to see.

There were two crowns on pillows on either side of the speaker – a Skybinder dressed in her formal robes. She even had a draping crown of pearls, I realized. That was a fortune in jewelry. Who was this Skybinder?

On either side of the dais, High'uns stood in their finery, looking dignified and proud. Where were they when we fought in these streets? Had they hidden in their well-defended homes? Had they been born here, like me, and simply didn't care how others suffered as long as they were comfortable, or had they arrived here later, looking on us as peasants beneath their feet?

"Buzz, cluster, group, sting,

The bees drive back the rest,

The bells of freedom ring,

They conquer and they best."

Odd that the Skybinder chose to read the third part of that odd poem-like prophecy. Usually, people didn't read that part. But Juste was beaming as her sing-song chant continued.

The wordless song of the choir accelerated, highlighting the momentousness of the moment.

Juste turned to me. "When we are crowned, you will wear the traditional winged crown and I shall wear the new symbol of our empire."

"We stand here today," the Skybinder intoned, her words carrying over the crowd. "To witness the crowning of the next ruler of what was once the Winged Empire and now will forever be known as the Empire of War and Wings."

My eyes went wide. He'd embraced the name our enemies gave us. He was taking it as his own.

"And we crown our Emperor, Lord of War – his snakes arriving as was prophesied so long ago, ushering in a new age, a new crown, and a new empire."

The snake crown. My eyes narrowed as I focused on it. Something tugged powerfully at my mind. A memory.

"And we crown his empress, subservient to him in every way, and yet a representation of the Wings that have forever served our great Empire."

How grand.

The choir hit a crescendo, soaring upward with ecstasy. The Skybinder raised her arms and the crowd roared.

I blinked twice and then the memory rushed up and swallowed me.

CHAPTER TWENTY

I knew it was one of the memories of the Hissan immediately.

"It's judgment," Frali said, shaking her raven hair and looking back at the small tangled mass that had once been a pool. "We have it deep in our hearts and we have it manifesting in the earth itself. A judgment on us for how we have walked on this earth."

I shook my head. "That doesn't make sense, Frali."

My voice was deep and rumbling.

"Doesn't it? We drove out all magic except that of the snake. We plucked mothers from children. Fathers from homes, never to return. We took all they owned and all they were and joined it to us."

"For good reason. All manifestations except snakes are abominations. And in other lands they do this. I have heard of one where they only manifest birds!" I shuddered at the thought.

"And now the earth has manifested," Frali said as if I hadn't even spoken. "It has manifested something to take back from us what we took. Or maybe just to take everything from everyone. All that pent up magic unloosed in the earth is angry. It wants to be let out to make and to heal, to rend and to create."

"Can you stop it?" I asked as the pool reached out and began to slowly wave its tentacles toward one of the trees growing along its edge. Already, it had conglomerated on a living tree until that tree was nothing but darkness and tangles like the pool.

"I can possibly manipulate it – for now – find ways to help us travel through it – to use it and be unaffected by it. Channel it into great works, maybe. But I cannot stop it. I can't see a way to do it."

"We could burn it."

"You know that's only temporary. We burned this pool seven days ago and now it is alive again."

I shook my head. "There has to be some way to stop it. Some way."

She began to shake her head but then her eyes rolled back into her head as they did when sometimes, the prophecy took her, and she said, "The joining of wing and snake shall be the end of the curse. From their pairing shall judgment be finally met, the price taken, the world set ablaze. From the crowning of the Adder and the Wing, and the spilling of their blood upon the heart of the tangle – one payment for guilt, one sacrifice to make us whole."

I surfaced, shaking my head of the memory, gasping at what I'd seen – at what that ancestor of the Hissan had said. I didn't fully understand, but the talk of payment, and judgment, and sacrifice worried me. I bit my lip.

I realized I was kneeling, facing Juste. He had his hands on both my arms, steadying me. He must have dropped me into this position while the memory rocked me. The Skybinder stood over us, intoning a blessing as the choir continued their wordless song.

"You remembered something," Juste said, his face very hard for someone who was getting everything he wanted.

"Where did your new crown come from?" I whispered.

"It was crafted for the Adder," he said, his eyes alight. "According to the specifications given to me by Ixtap before we parted."

That meant that he, Juste Montpetit, Le Majest of the Winged Empire, had been led on a merry chase by the Hissan. I wasn't sure exactly what the crown might do. It might kill him, leaving Ixtap to snatch up both the Winged Empire and the Far Stones. It might destroy the Forbidding – something I desperately needed right now with my family at its mercy. It would likely kill us both – based on the words of the prophecy I'd heard. I could warn Juste. Perhaps I even should.

I pressed my lips tightly together.

The wordless choir soared and above us, the Skybinder said, "And so, we honor you as our lord and emperor. May clear skies favor you and the land show you peace. May the sea calm for you and the people bow before you. And all the people said?"

And around us, the crowd replied, "Le Majest!" as they made the sign of the bird.

Juste's shoulders went just a little further back.

I should warn him. I should say something.

I bit the insides of my lips to keep them closed.

This was clearly a trap from the Hissan. And I didn't know what it might do or who it might hurt.

And yet, I wanted so badly to see him destroyed, to see him ruined forever, to see all this evil collapse in on itself. The fury I thought had abandoned me began to buzz again. With it, I could feel the hum of my bees. They were near. They were ready.

"And we also crown your empress, subservient to you, ruler

under your rule, joining together for the first time, land and air."

They laid the crowns on our heads at the same time and I said not a word.

CHAPTER TWENTY-ONE

Wind tore through the city, whirling through the crowd, carrying the brackish scent of the sea with it. There was a cry as one member of the chorus fell from the dais and above us, the Skybinder swayed in the wind. The strength of it nearly bowled me over, snatching my breath from me. Juste surged to his feet, pulling me with him. But he was looking in the wrong direction, facing the wind that came from the south of the city, when he should have been looking north through the city gate to where the Forbidding suddenly stilled.

I felt the voice in my head before I heard it.

JUDGMENT HAS COME WITHOUT MERCY.

And then everything was fire.

It seared across my vision and sent me to my knees. With it, my bee sent a frantic vision of Raquella, running through the Forbidding trail, the flames licking at her heels. It flicked to Osprey, eyes wide, mouth hanging open as the tentacles he was battling morphed into flame. It leapt to Ixtap looking out from the high towers of Kestrel City at the flames curling on the edge of the horizon.

Fire. Fire. Fire.

Heat.

Pain.

More fire.

I opened my eyes and Juste was shaking me.

"What have you done? What have you done?"

What had I done? I'd let him crown himself even though I knew it was a trap. Because I'd thought he was the only one who could be hurt by it. Shock left me wooden and paralyzed.

I opened my mouth, but no words came out of me.

Juste slapped me across the face – hard – and I fell forward without meaning to, my face slamming against his chest – my cheek right over where his feather was embedded.

Had I imagined it, or had it flared with warmth? Perhaps it was just the flames.

He shoved me off and I struggled to get up with my hands tied firmly behind my back. I was facing the gate side of the dais and the horror on the faces there seared me as much as the bright light of the flame did. People ran up and over each other like ants escaping their hill. The back row of seats was nothing more than ash and dust as the flames licked toward us.

Behind me, Juste was bellowing orders – orders for firefighting, orders to seal the gate, orders for those on the wall. His voice sounded frantic over the voices of so many others. No one was still. No one was waiting for anyone else to move.

My heart felt like it had stopped in my chest. Raquella. Osprey. My other siblings. The children.

Oh stars and skies, the children!

I was praying without knowing it, my lips flowing through the old prayer.

"Skies have mercy. Skies grant them peace. Hand of the almighty shelter them."

My vision stuttered and I was seeing through my bee's frenetic lens. He was trying to keep Raquella in view even as the flames licked at him. She sprinted just ahead of him, her back bright orange as the flames crept closer and closer. And then suddenly she was snatched up into the sky, talons wrapping around her shoulders.

Two dark spirit Ravens had her in their grasp as Victore rode on their shoulders – one foot on each back. Beside him, Wing Ivo rode Harpy, his eyes bright and desperate.

"Climb higher!" he roared. "Higher, Victore."

"Trouble. Misery. Hold on," Victore growled.

"You have the strength," Ivo called to him. "In the records, it says you carried four men out of battle when they were surrounded."

"Four," Victore muttered. "I don't remember."

"You don't have to remember," Ivo assured them as they soared upward. "You just need to let them remember."

I blinked and I was back in my body, struggling to my feet. The fire roared toward the city as the air from the sea rushed past to feed the flame. I tried to move and stumbled again to my knees. I felt a buzzing in my hand and opened my fist, twisting my head behind me to look. The bee who had been with Raquella lay crumpled in my hand.

I concentrated and absorbed it back inside. It had done well, but my heart was plummeting. I felt blind without my bees watching for me. Blind and deaf and frozen in terror.

Juste made a frustrated sound in the back of his throat, leaned over, and cut the bonds around my hands. "Stay close to me, Empress."

Claws formed up around us as if they could defend us from the madness of the flames. All I saw were blue backs as they hurried us to the carriage. Above us, Spirit birds flew frantically back and forth over the city.

Everything happened in a flurry of activity and just as I was tossed into the carriage I was rocked by another vision from my last bee.

He flew so erratically that it was hard to see clearly. The gusts of smoke and flame didn't help. And then I saw him. Osprey.

He was running through the Forbidding, the flames chasing after him. And he was on foot because in front of him Os flew low and grim, bigger than I'd ever seen him before. On his back and on his wings were balanced all my nieces and nephews, clutching each other with terror in their eyes.

I couldn't see my sisters or my in-laws. Fear clutched my heart and with it, a stabbing sense of pain and certainty. They would have gladly sent the children with Osprey if there was any chance of saving them. They would have gladly offered their own lives.

I was sobbing now, and hiccupping as the flames grew closer and closer, so close that they were licking the back of Osprey's clothes. Os couldn't hold him, too, and yet if he died in the flames, his magic would fade and the children would fall.

I gripped something – I didn't know what – with all my might and sobbed.

And for the first time, it wasn't fear or anger that welled up in me with the buzzing of the bees, it was pure, powerful love, soaring out from me and pouring through the bee that was tasked to watch Osprey.

“Please, please, please,” I begged my bees. “If I could have anything it would be this. Please, this one last thing.”

I concentrated on that one bee and focused all my longing, all my hope through his small frame and suddenly he was multiplying as my bees poured from him – rather than from me. They roared outward in a cloud, soaring toward Osprey and snatching him up from the flames in a swarm of coordinated bodies. They lifted him and carried him forward, toward Os, and then beside Os and together, the bird and the bees – one glowing purplish-white and the other a bright gold – lifted into the sky above the Forbidding, speeding over it.

There was a patch of green ahead and a town with a river. I could just make it out from here. Could they make it that far?

Flight of wind protect us, mercy of the skies fly over us, give us peace and protection, let us soar from this terror on the wings of eagles.

I gritted my teeth and forced every last ounce of energy I had into that prayer, into this magic, into all of it. Please, please hold on!

It was as if the folding of the undertrails was back, only instead of being folded inward, I was taking all that compression and spreading it outward, unraveling myself, my energy, my heart and my very soul for my little nieces and nephews and for Osprey. I was the swarm and the swarm was me – one in heart. One in spirit.

I could feel my bees fading as the town grew nearer. They dropped lower and lower over the waving tentacles of the Forbidding.

When, at last, Os passed us and set down in the town square, my heart squeezed with relief. My bees almost had Osprey there. Almost. They were growing weaker. He was just past the last reaching tentacle of Forbidding and dropping in height toward the town.

"Set me down," he commanded. "I can go on foot from here."

We hurried to lower him to the field and once he was on his own feet, he snatched one of my bees from the air and cupped it in his hand.

"I'm so sorry, House Apidae," he said with agonized eyes. "I could save only the children. I swear to you, I will protect them with my life. Not one will be lost."

Pain tore me from my vision, and I screamed as I lost hold of my bees and they vanished.

I looked up to see Juste with a red hand, looking down on me. He'd slapped me again. We were still surrounded by guards but in some kind of stable. Horses were being saddled and there was bustle all around us.

"Let's hope that was a Hissan memory and that you have something to share with me." The crown on his forehead slithered and moved as if it was alive. How was that even possible? I found my gaze riveted to it as he spoke. "No? What a shame. But either way, we cannot delay, Empress. You need to mount up. Don't worry about the dress. We'll bring things to change into."

"We're going somewhere?" I asked stupidly.

"To the Heart of the Forbidding," Juste said with blazing eyes. "I'm emperor now. Son of the gods. I will not allow an enemy like that to have purchase on my land."

"But it's on fire," I said, following him out of the coach to the horse a Claw walked over to me. The Claw grabbed my waist and boosted me into the saddle without so much as asking. My hand went up self-consciously to touch the crown on my head. Were we truly going to ride into those flames with crowns on our heads in fancy dress clothing? This was madness.

"You're the empress, darling," Juste said with a nasty smile. "You can't afford to let a little fire stop you now."

There was nothing to say to that. Because it was complete insanity.

I sat the mare, bit my lip, and prayed for my family. I did not know which of them lived and which of them had died, so I prayed for them all and hoped beyond hope that I would see them again.

My bees were worn out from saving Osprey and my family's little ones. I was surrounded by enemies. I had no plan for what was to come. But I was Aella and I was House Shrike and no matter what came next, I would be relentless.

***

Read the rest of Aella's story in Queen Magic, book five of Empire of War and Wings.

BEHIND THE SCENES:

USA Today bestselling author, Sarah K. L. Wilson loves spinning a yarn and if it paints a magical new world, twists something old into something reborn, or makes your heart pound with excitement ... all the better. Sarah hails from the rocky Canadian Shield in Northern Ontario – learning patience and tenacity from the long months of icy cold – where she lives with her husband and two small boys. You might find her building fires in her woodstove and wishing she had a dragon handy to light them for her

Sarah would like to thank Barbara, Melissa and Eugenia for their incredible work in beta reading and proofreading this book. Without their big hearts and passion for stories, this book would not be the same.

Sarah has the deepest regard for the talent of her phenomenal artist Luciano Fleitas who created the gorgeous cover art that accompanies this book. Without his work, it would be so much harder to show off this story the way it deserves. She also wants to thank her editor, Melissa, who tried her best to make this book better. Any errors remaining are all Sarah's.

Thanks also to the Noble Order of Female Fantasy Authors who keep me sane – sort of. And for my beloved husband, Cale and sons Neville and Leif who are endlessly patient as I talk to them about bookish passions.

Visit my website for more information:

www.sarahklwilson.com

www.ingramcontent.com/pod-product-compliance
Lightning Source LLC
Chambersburg PA
CBHW070538310726
48982CB00010B/1403/J

* 9 7 8 1 7 7 7 2 6 4 5 3 6 *